DATE DUE

SEP 27 '00			
DEC 19 '00			
MAR 0 8 2001			
NOV 1 0 2003			
DEC 0 8 2003			
SEP 2 9 2004			

FOLLETT

If That Breathes Fire,
We're Toast!

If That Breathes Fire, We're Toast!

Jennifer J. Stewart

Holiday House / New York

Library of Congress Cataloging-in-Publication Data
Stewart, Jennifer J.
If that breathes fire, we're toast! / by Jennifer J. Stewart.—1st ed.
p.   cm.
Summary: When eleven-year-old Rick and his mother move from San Diego to
Tucson he is not too happy about the change, but when they get a fire-breathing,
time-traveling dragon to replace their broken furnace, his new life starts to get
more interesting.
ISBN 0-8234-1430-2
[1. Dragons—Fiction.   2. Time travel—Fiction.   3. Moving, Household—
Fiction.   4. Arizona—Fiction.]   I. Title.
PZ7.S84895IF   1999
[Fic]—DC21   98-36883
CIP
AC

For my children,
who started it

Contents

Chapter 1

In Which I Leave
My Heart in San Diego

Thirty-four white cars in five minutes. That's when I knew for sure we weren't in California anymore.

"Doesn't anyone in Arizona drive a colored car?" I asked. It came out kind of whiny.

My mom glanced at me. I could see myself in her mirrored sunglasses, slumped down in my seat, my nose big enough for two people. "I thought you were still asleep," she said. I hadn't been. "It's just physics, Rick," she explained. "White cars don't heat up as much, and dark colors fade fast out here."

I looked away from the straight line of highway ahead of us to the "out here" whizzing by at a cruise-controlled seventy-five miles per hour. There wasn't much to recommend it, in my opinion. But then I hadn't been asked.

Reading my mind (which I wish she wouldn't do, but she's good at it), my mom said, "You'll get used to it. You may even like it."

"Mom?"

"Hmm?" She fiddled with the radio, trying to tune in a local station. Her finger hesitated over mariachi strains, then punched up Los Lobos singing their hearts out. She lowered the volume to hear me better.

"All those white cars."

She looked questioningly at me.

"They're all going the other way."

We sat in silence for a long time after that. Mom expects me to fit in, to find the beat right away. That's fine if you know how to dance, but my feet—sometimes I feel like they don't know which way to jump. And my sneakers. Boring, no brand name. No one would even *think* of swiping them.

I'm so average I could be in the *Guinness Book of World Records* if they had a category for it. Not too tall, not too short, dark hair, ditto eyes, ears that stick out, but not that much. Average. I'd lived in California all my life and liked it that way. I'd been looking forward to sixth grade because for that one year I'd be on top, king of the castle. But with this move, I'd have to start over at the bottom of the hill, stuck in some new school where everyone else had been best friends since before they learned to tie their shoes.

I felt as prickly as one of those two-ton cacti stretching its arms up to the sky.

We pulled up to the new house in Tucson, Arizona 85749, just at sunset—so brightly colored it looked fake. The house wore tired brown paint over stucco. It rambled in two directions like a low-slung shoe box with a porch hanging on the side for shade. A ring of rocks set off the "garden": a few shriveled cacti that hadn't seen rain since the conquistadores came through.

We stepped right into the living room. A fireplace curved like an eyeball watched us as we walked around. Kitchen and dining area were laid out to the left, bedrooms and a bathroom down the hall opposite. Our furniture sat right where the movers had dumped it, according to Mom's color-coded stickers. The couch looked lost, as if it didn't know where it belonged. I knew how it felt.

Mom ran back out to the van and came in carrying the phone. She plugged it into the kitchen jack and did a little dance when she got a dial tone.

I slid open the patio door and walked into the backyard. Traces of sunset still stained the sky to the west, although stars were popping out. I'd never seen so many stars. There weren't any outside lights and you couldn't see the city at all.

"Pizza's on its way," Mom announced, when I came back in. "Pepperoni, extra cheese. We can't cook until the gas company turns the gas on. Hard life, isn't it?" She twirled around. "So, what do you think?"

I just shrugged. I felt like I'd been planted on the moon. You'd have less space on a moon colony, though. Our old apartment could fit in here three times over, easy.

"You know," she said, looking at me from under her lashes, "this was once a bunkhouse. You know, history? The Wild West?"

I was interested in spite of myself. "A bunkhouse? What's that?"

"All the ranch hands lived here, kind of like a dormitory. If you look carefully you can tell where the doors were bricked over when the place was converted to a house, maybe thirty, forty years ago. See here." She traced an indentation in the plaster where a lintel had been, sliding her finger down the side of a once-upon-a-time door.

Possible cowboy leftovers, I don't know, maybe rusty branding irons or old bottles hazing violet in the sun, could be waiting to be found. By me. Maybe there'd be a horseshoe I could nail over the door. Weren't they supposed to bring good luck? I could use some.

Fat Boy woke me in the morning by jumping on my chest and purring. He sounds like a Harley

4

motorcycle revving up. I listened hard, but couldn't hear any other sound. Unused to silence, I didn't feel comfortable. I got up, clutching twenty pounds of cat to my chest for protection.

There was a note on the kitchen table. "Dropping off my business card and sample shots," Mom had written. "Back late morning. Expect someone from Southwest Gas to inspect the furnace, etc., around 10?" Then she'd hastily added a PS: "Check his ID before you let him in." Didn't she know I was almost twelve? We'd done stranger danger in kindergarten.

Rummaging around, I found milk and juice in the fridge. The Cheerios were on the counter, but I could only find paper plates, no bowls. So I drank my cereal and washed it down with orange juice, adding a glass of water. I didn't want to dry up and blow away like those tumbleweeds we saw along the highway. The water tasted fine. I mean, it didn't have a taste. San Diego *agua* tastes like it's been filtered through steel wool before they add the chlorine to kill the bugs. You can smell it when you turn on the faucet.

Tiles cool under my bare feet, I headed down the hall past my mom's bedroom, darkroom, and office, in that order, before reaching the bathroom and my room at the tail end. I didn't waste any time getting dressed. There was this weird tree growing outside my window. It had a pale green trunk and itty-bitty leaves. Everything was really quiet except for this strange buzzing coming from dozens of kamikaze beetles with iridescent green bellies zooming around the trunk. The August heat pushed its way in, reaching out to mummify me, so I shut the window.

Then I spent some time opening boxes and getting out my stuff, stowing my wet suit and Boogie board way in the back of the closet. Not much chance, actually zilch, I'd find a place to use them here. My shell and sea glass collection went on the top shelf of my bookcase. Then I remembered and left room for cowboy leftovers.

Ed Wallace (his name embroidered above the breast pocket of his shirt and printed on his ID) replaced the cover on the old furnace, then rocked back on his heels, absently wiping his grimy fingers on his pants. Snapping off his flashlight, he turned to me.

"Afraid it's done for, son. Belts shot, burners warped. You'll never get it lit." He winked at me. "And if you did, I wouldn't go smoking any cigars around here. Might maybe explode. I'm surprised an old monster like this still exists."

Right then the front door opened and I heard my mom's heels clicking on the tile, so old Ed had to explain it all over again, not that I totally got it the first time. I'm not real mechanical. While he talked, I started checking out the cobwebs around the ductwork. Arizona has creepy bugs, besides plants with stickers. There are scorpions and brown recluse spiders, also the black widow, a real bad-news spider with a red hourglass on her stomach: One bite and you're dead meat. We have those in California, too. My mom doesn't like anything with more than four legs. A scorpion skittering across the floor would be a point for my side, though it would take more than that to send her packing.

My mom was saying that she really hoped the furnace might be jury-rigged, at least for one more winter.

Ed shook his head. "You'll have to get a new one," he said decidedly. "And if you need a recommendation—"

"Wait a second," I said. I'd noticed an old label on the side of the furnace and carefully peeled it off. "Take a look at this, Mom." I read it aloud. "'Dragonwerks, Ltd. Lifetime Guarantee. Replacement Dragon.' There's even an address." I handed Mom the label with its stylized dragon curled around old-fashioned writing.

The gas man scratched his forehead. "I don't know, Mrs. Morales. I've never heard of Dragonwerks. It could be they went under long ago. There's more efficient units available, that I do know, and they're smaller and put out more heat."

"It might be worth a try, though," I said.

"I won't have the money to put in a whole new system until my business gets going," admitted my mom. "If I can replace it for free . . ."

"Couldn't hurt," agreed Ed. "Here's my number if it doesn't work out." He handed her his business card. "Anyways, you've got time. You're looking at three, maybe four months before it gets cold enough you even need gas heat."

He must have been joking. I bet it never gets that cold here.

"Ma, have you unpacked the camping stuff yet?"

"Most of it's there, under the phone." She pointed to a large box doing double duty as a desk.

I opened the box and groped around inside, grabbing what I wanted. Then on to the fridge, collecting an egg as my booty, and out the front door.

I was ready for a scientific *eggs*-periment. I found a sunny spot—there's no lack in Tucson, Arizona—and put the iron skillet on the ground. Deftly I cracked the egg one-handed into the skillet and checked my watch for the start time. Accurate records are important. My mom had shown me the skin index in the newspaper, where it tells you how long you can stay outside at different times of the day before being fried. I could argue all I wanted that that index was for Anglos, not me, but I didn't get very far. Mom was making a religion out of wearing sunscreen and wanted me to keep the faith. Anyway, that gave me the idea.

Just then a girl pedaled up on a purple bicycle she'd outgrown. When she saw me, she skidded to a stop, raising dust with her high tops.

"Watcha doing?" she asked, unbuckling her helmet. She pulled it off, revealing flattened straw-colored hair tied back in a ponytail. Her blue eyes took in me, the skillet, and the egg.

I picked out a piece of sun-baked weed from the egg white before answering. "I heard in Tucson it's hot enough to fry eggs on the sidewalk, but (a) there isn't any sidewalk, and (b) it's not sanitary. It's going pretty slowly though."

"I have an idea," the girl said. She swung her backpack off her shoulder, unzipped it, and rummaged around. She pulled out and discarded two Phillips-head screwdrivers, an Allen wrench, a couple of spark plugs, and what looked like a turkey baster but maybe wasn't. Eventually she located a magnifying glass and offered it to me. "This might work."

"Thanks," I said. The bottom of the egg was starting to cook now, but the top was still watery. I lined up the magnifying glass with the sun and focused its rays on the yolk.

"My little brother used to burn bugs with it, until my mom made him stop," she offered. "You just moved in, didn't you?"

"Yeah, me and my mom." I kept moving the magnifying glass so the egg wouldn't cook all in one spot. "We're from San Diego."

"My friends are there right now, on vacation," the girl said. "My name's Natalie. Natalie Randall. I live at the end of the street, past the park." She pointed behind her. "Why'd you come here?"

I shrugged. "Back home my mom worried I'd join a gang or something. But the closest I got to a gang was the chess club at school."

When Natalie laughed, sunlight glinted off her braces. "We've got a chess club at our school, too. I'm going into sixth grade in a couple of weeks."

"Me, too," I said.

"Maybe we'll be in the same class." She looked a lot more enthusiastic than I felt. "I hope you like your egg well done."

The egg was smoking. It didn't look good.

"I'm not sure even Fat Boy would touch that."

"Who's Fat Boy?"

"He's our cat," I told her. "You can come in and meet him if you like."

"Okay," said Natalie. She leaned her bike against the house and set her backpack down beside it. It clanked.

Gingerly I tested the skillet handle. I had to wrap part of my T-shirt around it before I could pick it up.

Fat Boy wouldn't come out from under my bed, not even for a can of Fishy Feast. He backed away further when I showed him the egg. He wasn't adjusting well to the move. I gave up and stuck the pan in the sink to soak.

Natalie and I went to check out the backyard. A hammock with a couple of busted strings hung between two rough-barked trees with microscopic leaves. The hammock's dust made me sneeze, but it swung okay. The yard had these trees—Natalie called them mesquites—along with some low cacti called prickly pears. An old barbed-wire fence surrounded our property. Here and there the wire had sprung loose and lay curled up rusting on the ground. We scared up a few brown rabbits with white tails like cotton balls.

Natalie informed me that if I ever got lost in the desert without water, I could just slice open a cactus and suck on the juices. "'Course, you'd have to be pretty desperate."

I'm the one who found the horseshoe tracks. The ground must have been wet once and the shoes bit in deep. Natalie said if we didn't have any rain soon, they'd probably fossilize like dinosaur footprints. I laughed. I didn't find a horseshoe, but maybe I'd found a friend, even if she was a girl.

"I got Dragonwerks on the phone," Mom announced at dinner. "I talked to the funniest person. She wanted to know everything about us, how long we'd lived here, if it was just the two of us. I must have talked to her for twenty minutes."

I helped myself to seconds of frijoles and a tortilla. "So, will they be sending us a new furnace?"

"Yes, and that was another strange thing. She wanted to know the year and make of the one we have. Wouldn't you think they'd just send the latest model? Anyway, that's what I told her, but she said the newest dragons weren't ready, 'not hatched yet.' I suppose that means they're still on the drawing board. She's sending me a reconditioned one in the meantime, a 'temporary dragon,' she called it."

"I hope that's okay," I said doubtfully. I knew about reconditioned cars.

"It's free. I'm not complaining. I'll have to pay for the installation, of course, but that should be nothing compared to the cost of a new unit. I was counting on painting the house with the money I've got set aside. Let's hope we don't have to replace everything. You know what I told her? I told her I didn't so much need a dragon as a fairy godmother." She sighed. Mom had spent the whole day unpacking and that could make you desperate for a real live human to talk to. But telling our life story to a complete stranger?

"Everything else works, though, doesn't it?" I wanted someone else to take the house off our hands when the time came. "The house just needs, what is it you tell your photo makeover ladies?"

"Some new eye shadow to catch the light?" Mom laughed and shook her head. "I'm afraid this house needs more than cosmetics, Rick. More like plastic surgery." She stirred her beans with her fork, swirling the melting cheese. "Oh, well. It was a good deal and the most I could afford."

Temporarily I called off my campaign of going back to San Diego. I could wait.

"Don't go apologizing on me, Mom. I never had my own room before. I bet you'll be booking weddings right and left once your ad comes out."

Mom raked her fingers through her short dark hair. "The ads will bring in business, but since most people plan weddings months in advance, we may have to wait a while for any money. Don't you worry though, kid—that's my job. I won't be breaking into your piggy bank. At least, I hope not." She shot me a rueful smile. "Soon as school starts in a few weeks you'll meet more kids. What's the name of the girl you met today? Does she have any brothers or sisters?"

"Natalie. She has one little brother. He's five. She has to watch him sometimes. They've got a pool." That kind of balanced things out, I guessed.

"Speaking of water, you wash, I dry? Or I dry, you wash?"

It was her little joke. Don't flip coins with my mom.

"Sure," I said. As we did the dishes we looked out at the rainbow-sherbet sunset. Maybe living on the moon wouldn't be so bad after all.

Chapter 2

Dragonwerks Delivers

"Ready, Rick?"

"Just about," I answered, my voice muffled under the catcher's mask. I pulled the oven mitts over my long-sleeved shirt. They went almost to my elbows. Already sweat was beading up on my forehead, threatening to trickle down my nose.

I slipped into the bathroom and closed the door. Fat Boy hissed at me from the defensive position he'd taken behind the toilet. The cage to carry him to the vet lay open on the counter next to the sink. I moved in closer, bumping my mom.

"Maybe you'd better let me handle this, ma'am," I said, doing my best John Wayne imitation.

Mom hesitated, glancing down at her bare legs. Fat Boy hissed again. "I'll scoot," she said gratefully. "Call me when you're ready."

I reached for Fat Boy and the cat dug his claws into the oven mitt.

"Okay, *gato,* you force me to use the secret weapon." I reached up and flushed. The noise so scared Fat Boy that he jumped right into my arms. The cage door was latched before the toilet finished gurgling.

I opened the door wide. "No need to thank me, ma'am. Just doin' my job."

"My hero," Mom said. She hammed it up, batting her eyelashes at me. "I think I can take it from here."

"Sure you don't want me along? You might need some help getting him back in there."

"Naw, he's such a pussycat after his shot, he can't wait to get back in the cage to go home. But *gracias.*" She lifted up the catcher's mask and gave me a quick kiss on the cheek. "Get that stuff off before you die of heat exhaustion."

Fat Boy's rabies shot was due, plus Mom needed to talk to the vet about Fat Boy's "adjustment problem." She'd caught him spraying the drapes twice already.

It was five days after the move. Nothing much to report beyond that. Well, I'd gone swimming at Natalie's twice, but I wasn't ready to be best friends with a girl. Still, she was okay. Natalie had a workshop all to herself—she and her dad built it out of hay bales and stuccoed it, and he helped her wire it for electricity. She told me she goes there to think and get away from her brother, Ben. Also she likes to take things apart and put them back together. They usually work after she tinkers with them. I had given her my clock radio, which got banged around during the move, and the next day she had it working.

Soon after Mom left for the vet, Fat Boy meowing piteously, the Roadway Freight Express guy dropped off a big wooden crate. It had Dragonwerks' logo stamped on the side and also "Fragile: Handle with Care" labels plastered all over. I signed for my mom. The crate wouldn't fit through the door without taking off the hinges, so the Freight Express guy and I trundled the crate on a dolly around back and set it on the porch. It would be safely in the shade come afternoon. Natalie had warned me that heat could really do a number on electronics. "Solid-state can get solidly melted," was how she put it.

As if I had conjured her with my thought, just then Natalie rode up. "What's cookin' today?" For once she was minus her backpack, so she didn't have a hammer handy. It didn't take too long to find Mom's toolbox, though. When you live with another person for as long as I have, you get to know how she thinks. Mom had left the toolbox by the shower as a reminder to tackle the dripping showerhead.

Well, I could be handy, too.

Outside again, I took the claw end of the hammer and began prying at the lid of the crate. It was going to be an ordeal. Someone had sunk four-inch nails in all the way around.

"As if Dragonwerks didn't want anything to get in," said Natalie.

"As if they didn't want anything to get out," I joked.

Finally the last nail screeched out its surrender, sounding like five fingernails on a blackboard. It was the only time I'd shivered since getting to Arizona.

Natalie began removing packing straw. It was real straw, not those little Styrofoam peanuts. Pretty soon she had uncovered the top of the furnace. I didn't know exactly what I was expecting to see, but wouldn't a furnace be shaped like a box? This was more like a tube, fat in the middle, like an overstuffed burrito. And it wasn't painted gray. It was green. Lime green. Had someone messed up the order?

"Let's get the end off, then," I said. Natalie picked up the hammer. We got the front panel off.

The green metal began to heat up in the sun. I reached in to grab more packing straw.

Wait a minute. It moved.

It couldn't have. I rubbed my eyes. It must be the heat. I started in on the straw again.

But there—it moved again. It could be sun-stroke. Mom was right. I should have worn a hat.

It was not my imagination. The packing straw rustled.

"Did you see that?" I whispered.

"Yeah," Natalie whispered back. "It's moving."

It was moving, just a little, in rhythm, like a sleeping person's chest. Whatever was in there was alive. We both stepped backward.

"What is it?" Natalie asked, goggle-eyed.

"You look."

"Uh-uh, not me. You do it. It's yours, whatever it is."

Suddenly the metal thing heaved and pitched forward.

Natalie and I ran. We squeezed in behind a saguaro cactus.

The thing shrugged off the rest of the straw, the way a dog shakes off water, then opened its mouth and yawned. Its mouth was filled with pointed teeth.

"What is it?" Natalie asked again.

We could now see the creature clearly. Its eyes were ruby red, maybe ten times as large as a cat's, topped with long spiky eyelashes. It wore dangly fire-opal earrings. Although it was the size of a large dog, it was shaped more like a fat cigar, with a tail as long as its body ending in a wicked-looking barb. On its back were what looked like black umbrellas, but these now unfurled into small but serviceable wings, as the whatever-it-was stretched. It also had shimmery green scales, the size of cucumber slices. The creature stretched like Fat Boy after a long nap, first arching its back up, then down.

"It's—it's not a furnace," I said finally.

"Well, no," conceded the creature in a low raspy voice. "But you did order a replacement dragon."

It could talk! I couldn't. My mouth hung open.

Natalie elbowed me out of the way, her curiosity overcoming her fear. "You're a dragon?"

"At your service." She, it had to be a she, held out her wings like the skirts of a dress, sinking down into a kind of curtsy.

My voice came back, though it squeaked a little. "You're supposed to be a dragon *furnace*," I said. "The guy from the gas company said our old one had to go. He said it was a real dragon, a monster." I babbled but couldn't seem to stop. In old movies, if you keep the villain talking he won't shoot you. Probably we looked snack-size to the dragon.

The dragon broke in. "Tact is obviously not your strong point. . . . Well, we'll just have to make the best of it. I don't think a mistake has been made. All the papers were in order. Some children, you know, need fairy godmothers. *Others* need dragons."

Just then the mail van drove up, forestalling further questions. The carrier called out to me, "I have a package here for your mother." He hopped out and handed it to me, then jumped back into his van, completely ignoring the dragon. He would have tripped over her tail, if she hadn't twitched it out of his way.

"How come he didn't see you?" Natalie asked. Her eyes were round, but her breathing was starting to slow back down.

The dragon examined her lacquered nails, or maybe you'd call them claws, for imperfections. "Many people don't go looking for dragons, you know. They don't believe we exist, and really, for that kind, we don't. Unless, not to put too fine a point on it, I choose to make them believe—I suppose it's a sort of reverse camouflage? Sometimes it's better to remain unseen." The dragon blew smoke out her nostrils and disappeared in the haze. Then, just as suddenly, she reappeared, like a slide coming into focus. "Also, I must admit our numbers have dwindled," she continued, not missing a beat. "The usual culprits." Here the dragon ticked them off. "Destruction of habitat, disruption of the food chain . . . far fewer princesses to make a meal of . . . Too many imitations, of course. They act like princesses, but they aren't the same." Here she paused to sigh. "It's like saccharin—it doesn't really taste as sweet. I detest artificial flavorings." She surveyed us, Natalie in her T-shirt and flowered bike shorts, me in a striped T over baggy jeans shorts. "You aren't related to royalty, are you?"

"No," I said quickly. "Common as grubs, Mom always says."

"Me too," added Natalie.

"Pity," said the dragon. "I *am* rather hungry. I've been in that crate for several days."

Natalie kicked me in the ankle.

"Ow! I mean, oh," I said. "Maybe you'd like a sandwich? Peanut butter and jelly okay?"

"That sounds lovely," said the dragon. "Perhaps I should introduce myself. My name is Madam Yang."

We told her our names. I held the door open for the dragon and invited her into the kitchen. I quickly made three sandwiches and poured milk, too, for good measure. It seemed a smart policy to keep the dragon well fed. We all sat down around the table.

"I forgot to ask if you like your bread toasted. Sorry."

The dragon picked up her sandwich, considering. Then she exhaled and a thin orange flame shot out of her mouth, browning the bread. She nibbled delicately. We waited while she ate. She seemed to have some trouble with the peanut butter sticking her mouth together. I thought about that tube of superglue biding its time in my mom's toolbox. It might come in handy.

"In pictures, you know, dragons are always much bigger," Natalie observed.

The dragon set down the crusts on her plate and wiped her mouth before replying. "Good public relations, mostly. The knights in armor did like to look brave for their official portraits. It's not surprising that court painters would indulge them and exaggerate the size of their foes, but it's true, we were bigger once upon a time, as stories go. Then there's evolution. Once humans invented gunpowder and so on, survival depended more on the ability to hide than being able to peel off a suit of armor quickly."

"But couldn't you just go invisible?" I asked.

"It's not exactly sporting, is it, Rick? Especially when people quit wearing armor—regretfully, I never did get to try out that new can opener I invented. . . . Besides, disappearing takes massive amounts of skill and concentration, plus you have to hold your breath. Where was I? Oh, yes. The smaller you are, the easier it is to hide, you see. I am actually on the large side, for a fully grown dragon."

"How old are you?" I asked—then thought, perhaps I should have kept my mouth shut. Some people don't like to tell. Maybe that was true of dragons as well.

But she didn't seem offended. "Close to five hundred years old, I should say, or perhaps I shouldn't. I don't like to boast."

"What about unicorns?" Natalie asked, still curious.

"What about them? Oh, I see. Well, the story is pretty much the same, except as prey rather than predator, if you catch my drift; far fewer have survived, unfortunately. But again, you have to be looking. They don't just walk up and ring your doorbell on Halloween night."

Natalie's eyes widened. "But where would you find them?"

"I don't like to tell tales," said the dragon. "Don't you have a public library? You can look these things up, can't you?"

I heard a car door slam.

"Quick! We've got to hide you!"

We shooed Madam Yang into my room. Mom being the creative type, I knew she'd spot the dragon, even if the mailman hadn't a clue. And the practical side of her wouldn't think a dragon was a good idea. She'd have the Roadway Freight Express guy back here and that crate marked "Return to Sender" in a minute. But so far that dragon was the most interesting thing that had happened to me, and I wasn't about to let her go. Even if she did talk to me like some grouchy great-aunt.

Mom came in the door lugging the cat carrier. She set it down on the floor and opened the latch. Fat Boy stalked out. He headed toward the kitchen and his food dish, to make sure it hadn't moved.

"I'm sorry I took so long," Mom was saying. "I got to talking with Dr. Cotter about an idea of mine, glamour shots for pets. He thinks there might be a real market. I mean, if I can do proms, why not poodles? I'll take some snaps of Fat Boy and make up a flyer. Can you see it: Glamour Puss?"

Natalie thought it was a really radical idea. I signaled her to keep my mom talking, usually not a problem. Anyway, anyone could tell she was really excited. I headed down the hall to check on our guest.

Fat Boy trailed me, licking his whiskers, his tail curved in a question mark. He paused at the bedroom door and sniffed. But when he saw the dragon on my bed, he puffed up like a blowfish and bolted.

"But maybe I'll wait till Fat Boy's in a better mood," I heard my mom say. "The vet says it takes a while for a cat to get comfortable in a new place. Look, here's Dr. Cotter's business card. Isn't that a great logo shot with the Great Dane licking his ear?"

I put a finger to my lips. The dragon looked at me, but she obligingly curled up on my bed. I closed the door to my room.

"Ma, Natalie and I were going to ride over to the library. That okay?"

"Sure. You want me to drive you?"

That was an absolutely fantastic idea. This way we wouldn't be leaving Mom alone with the dragon. I wasn't sure I could trust Madam Yang yet and didn't want Mom coming unglued or worse. Around dragons, dismemberment happens.

I peeked in my room again. Madam Yang was examining my Walkman. She had slipped the headphones over her ears, but upside down so they looked like a stethoscope. She pressed the ON button with one claw. Her eyes bugged out and she ripped the headphones off. The twang and crash of heavy metal was perfectly audible to me.

"Crank the volume down," I said. "Okay, we're going to the library. Don't go anywhere. Please!"

The dragon nodded, but I wasn't sure she heard me. She'd found the volume control. The head-phones were back on and she was swaying to the beat when I left.

Call me a coward, but I wished I could lock the door.

In the library, Natalie introduced me to the children's librarian, Ms. Marcella Mortenson. She had spiky blonde hair and Buddy Holly-style glasses, which slid down her thin nose but never quite off it. Her eyes were sharp, especially when I told her what kind of books I wanted.

She led me to a computer terminal and tapped out the subject query, her long blue fingernails clicking on the keys. I had to watch her closely; she said she'd only show me once. Dragons were in the 398s, with other mythological beasts. It made me wonder how many other "myths" aren't. Aren't myths at all, I mean.

Soon I had a pile of books, from animal folk-lore to mythology. As I expected, there wasn't much hard evidence, mostly lots of accounts about knights and damsels in distress. St. George and the dragon figured in a lot of artwork. What Madam Yang had said about official portraits got me thinking. The dragon hadn't fared too well in that particular fight, and the painters and sculptors all had definitely sided with St. George. If he were alive today, he'd be doing product endorsements for sure. I settled on five books and took them up to the counter. Before I got my new library card, Marcella lectured me about not turning down corners on the pages of books or marking my place with Popsicle sticks. I promised I wouldn't. I mean, I wouldn't dare.

"Interested in dragons, hmm?" said the librarian.

"Yes, I am. I'd like to find out all I can about them."

"Try Chinese mythology," the librarian recommended, and she surrendered the card.

I quickly marched back to the computer and located one more book.

"Three weeks," Marcella warned me. "Don't be late."

Not on your life. She tucked a free bookmark inside the front cover before handing the book to me.

"Now, that's a *real* dragon," I told Natalie when we were headed back in the van. She gave me a funny look, like she couldn't decide whether I needed to be kicked again.

"The best librarians often are," my mom offered lightly.

Chapter 3

Damsel Distressed

I slipped the dragon more peanut butter sandwiches for insurance purposes before crawling into bed. Madam Yang's red eyes glowed eerily from my closet. I thought about asking my mom for a night-light, but I hadn't used one since I was six. And although she'd understand about feeling strange in a new place, I definitely didn't want her going up to the closet to show me nothing was hiding there, like she did when I was little. Because there *was* a monster in my closet. So I kept quiet.

In the morning, I felt extremely relieved—I had everything I'd gone to sleep with: fingers, toes, nose, etcetera. Mom had appointments with the directors of some private schools in the area, hoping to get their school-pictures business. I practically shoved her out the door. Natalie zipped over as soon as it was polite. Madam Yang didn't look like a morning creature and wasn't too communicative until we got a couple cups of coffee in her.

Natalie couldn't contain herself. "Come on, Madam Yang, what can you do?"

Dragons are mysterious creatures. I think they like being mysterious. The dragon ignored Natalie's question and began picking her teeth with the tip of one of her talons. Maybe this is polite in dragon society, but it looked rude.

We had skimmed the library books, checking out the pictures and stopping to read where it looked interesting. I learned you were luckiest if you were born in the year of the blue dragon. A blue dragon child supposedly combines the best of everything: looks, talent, personality, you name it. Of course, Natalie and I turned out to be cows: kind, stubborn, honest creatures that go "moo" and jump over the moon if startled. It could have been worse, though. If we had had January or early February birthdays before the Chinese New Year, we would have been rats. But beyond that, as far as getting some concrete useful information about my particular dragon, the books didn't help.

So I decided to join Natalie in badgering Madam Yang, now that she looked more awake.

"Yeah, can you grant wishes?" I asked.

"Do I look like a genie? You've been myth-informed. Humans," the dragon sniffed, "never know anything. Look, there's magic all around you. Even the past is all around you. All you have to do is scratch beneath the surface of the present."

"I don't get you."

"I forgot, humans don't see anything but what's in front of them. Come outside and I'll show you."

I held the screen door open for Madam Yang and Natalie. The dragon put her nose to the ground in a few spots, then hesitated for a few moments and appeared to listen. She led us practically to the end of the backyard, up to the barbed-wire fence, then stopped and sat on her haunches.

"Here," she said, pointing. "Something happened here. I can smell it. Anger smells like hot tar, happiness more like—"

"Sunshine on spring flowers?" I dared.

The dragon narrowed her eyes at me. "Try peanut butter. Put your hand down," she ordered.

I put my hand on the ground. It felt like dirt. Just dirt. Okay, hot dirt. It didn't feel like the past or the future or magical in any way.

"What does it feel like?" asked Natalie.

I looked at Madam Yang. "Gritty," I said.

The dragon sniffed again. "Natalie, move back. You're crowding Rick." She turned those stoplight eyes on me. "And, Rick, you have to concentrate. Your emotions are what's important. Using your feelings as a catalyst, you can slip in and out of time." She scored the dirt with her claws and dug down about four inches. The bottom of the hole was black. "What you see are the remains of a long-ago fire. Put your hand there and think hard."

I put my hand in the hole and closed my eyes. Nothing happened at first, but gradually the dirt under my fingers, which had been relatively cool at first, started heating up. It got so hot I had to snatch my hand out and blow on it. Madam Yang must have been playing a trick on me, breathing fire when I wasn't looking.

Then I opened my eyes. The stars were out. The moon was just climbing up over the ridge. And that was really weird, since my watch called it ten o'clock in the morning. The second hand had stopped. In front of me glowed red-orange coals from a fire that should have been long dead. *Had* been long dead just a few seconds ago. There was a branding iron resting against the ring of stones.

Natalie was nowhere.

The dragon's teeth glowed in the firelight, like the Cheshire cat's. Only with fangs. I shivered, though not from cold.

"Where am I?"

"The question should be, *when* are you? You're in the same place."

Over my shoulder, the bunkhouse cast a long, low shadow. Light leaked out one of the windows, but the light was different, somehow softer. It wasn't electricity, that's for sure.

"I don't like this," I said. "I want to go back."

"You can't," said Madam Yang patiently. "At least not yet. You have to wait for the fire to die down, otherwise your hand will get burned."

"Where's Natalie?"

"Natalie will be there when we get back. But first, a little investigation's in order. As long as we're here, let's see what's going on up at the ranch."

"What ranch?"

"I would guess that way." She pointed.

I couldn't see anything except the soft glow of light on the horizon, but suddenly I could hear something. Slow, kind of soppy music played on guitars, the soft notes blurring together. We began walking toward the sound.

It was farther than I thought. Sound carried along the dry riverbeds. Wait a minute, the arroyo was running. Cool water tumbled over rocks, respectable enough to be called a *rillito* if not an actual river. I wanted to explore further, but Madam Yang pulled at my shirt.

"Remember, Rick, I sniffed out strong emotion. We may not have much time."

I stopped. "Just exactly what emotion did you sniff out?"

She smiled that mysterious dragon smile of hers, but didn't answer me. Oh, great! Here I was stranded in time with a dragon who was playing mind games with me. I thought about refusing to go on, but figured she might take a chunk out of me if I hesitated.

After we'd walked ten, fifteen minutes, we came upon an adobe wall, head high. On the other side I could see the tops of trees and colored lanterns. People were talking over the music, though their words escaped me. Farther along the wall was a wooden gate. I tried to peer in but had to duck my head out of the way when the gate suddenly swung open.

"Dios mio," someone muttered. "I thought I'd never get away." The girl turned and would have walked right into me. Instead she stifled a scream and grabbed my arm.

"Please, don't make a noise. Did Roberto send you? Take me to the horses."

She wore a long white dress that drooped off her shoulders. Tiers of lace ruffles cascaded downward, making her look like an over decorated wedding cake. Her only jewelry was a saint's medal on a gold chain. If I had to guess, I'd say she was several years older than me, maybe sixteen or seventeen. She wore her dark hair piled high on the back of her head, with small scented white flowers braided into the coils.

"No, Roberto didn't send me." I automatically answered her in Spanish. I hadn't spoken it on a regular basis since my *abuela* Josefina died, but it all came back.

She squeezed my arm and marched me away from the gate, pleading in a whisper, *"Por favor—*

please don't tell my uncle. I've got to escape. Quickly, before they miss me at the fiesta."

Behind us the gate creaked open again. A man stepped out. He had on a fancy outfit like the *charros* you see on mariachi music specials on public television, tight pants and a matching short jacket over a white ruffled shirt. The outfit didn't suit him; he carried too much weight. He looked like Fat Boy in doll's clothes. He took out a handkerchief and dabbed delicately at his nose.

"Atanacia!" he called out in a nasal voice. "Atanacia, are you there?"

The girl beside me shivered. I couldn't tell if it was from fear or disgust. "My cousin Eduardo! My uncle wants us to marry. But I love Rober— another. Eduardo must not find us here together. Please, please, bring the horses to the small corral," she begged. "I will slip out again when the musicians break."

Before I could respond, she turned and swished away, her skirts billowing out.

"Eduardo, I'm here, just getting some air. Let's go back in together, shall we?" Atanacia tucked her arm in his and they went back inside. As the gate swung shut I heard her say she had saved a dance for him.

I stood there like a fool and hoped I blended in with the desert plants. Madam Yang tugged on my pants leg.

"Come on, let's get the horses," she hissed.

"But—"

"If ever I saw a damsel in distress, she's one. You're no knight, but you're all she's got. Come on!"

I trotted after Madam Yang, trying to make sense of the situation. If Atanacia was the damsel in distress and I was supposed to be the knight . . . "Uh, Madam Yang, you wouldn't be thinking of eating her, would you?"

"Don't be silly. Atanacia was dust and bones long ago. I like my meals fresh."

I stopped in my tracks. "You mean we're going to help a . . . a . . . ghost?"

"Well, she's not dead yet, not now anyway, but she might as well be, if we don't help her. We've got to find out what's happened to Roberto and the horses!"

Chapter 4

Meanwhile, Back at the Ranch

We had no idea who Roberto was, what he looked like, or where we would find him, but locating the horses turned out to be a no-brainer; we just followed our noses. We found two horses saddled up and ready to go tethered outside a small corral, not too far from the bunkhouse, which we were careful to circle around. Five or six other horses were milling around inside the corral. When I got too close, one stuck its big velvety nose on my shirt and snuffled around, sliming me. It lost interest when it discovered I didn't have anything horsy to eat in my pockets. Madam Yang and I didn't see anyone, and if Roberto was hiding close by, he didn't come out when we called softly. I even hissed out Atanacia's name like a password but no dice.

"Let's check back at the bunkhouse," said Madam Yang. "Maybe Roberto is one of the ranch hands."

That made some kind of sense, though not a lot did at this point. But, assuming Roberto had saddled the horses, we just might find him with the other cowboys.

By this time the moon was up and my eyes adjusted. I found my way back to the bunkhouse without getting tripped up and landing in some cactus.

Dark curtains covered most of the bunkhouse windows, but at the last one we got lucky. Someone had stuffed a rag into the window where a pane had cracked or broken. Cautiously I pulled it out and looked into my own bedroom as it was many years ago.

A young man strained at the ropes tying him to a chair in the center of the room. A purple bruise decorated one cheek, above the gag. Perhaps this was Roberto? A low bed and a table completed the sparse furnishings. For a second, I didn't see the room's only other occupant, though he was seated right under my nose. I looked down on a bald head, a curling mustache a little lower, then noticed the pistol held negligently in his hands.

"You don't have to worry," the guard was saying. "Don Carlos doesn't want you removed permanently, least as long as you don't cause any more trouble. You should be thankful for that.

All we have to do is sit out the party. After the announcement of the engagement's made, you're free to go." He shifted his weight trying to get comfortable and the chair creaked. "And if I were you, boy, I'd make tracks and never look back. Don Carlos doesn't like to be crossed."

"What's going on?" whispered Madam Yang impatiently. "I can't see."

I shushed her and we pulled back to the nearest tree.

"There's a guy with a gun and another guy tied up in a chair." I said it matter-of-factly, but my voice squeaked. "I don't suppose we could go home now?"

Madam Yang just looked at me. I got a grip and explained the layout.

The dragon nodded her head. "The man tied in the chair—that would be Roberto, I fear. Fortunately, I have an idea. You go up and knock on the door."

I stared at her. "What kind of plan is that? I'm going to get shot!"

"No, you won't—well, I don't think you will. Just trust me. Get him to open the door, and I'll do the rest."

No one could make me like it, but Madam Yang was the only familiar thing in this whole unfamiliar time. Trust her, she said. So what else could I do? Hide, run away, go back to California and join the gold rush, if I hadn't missed it, see

San Francisco burn down in the great earthquake of 1906, if I lived long enough . . . and never see my mom again . . . though maybe I'd have a chance of meeting up with some of my great-great-great-grandparents. The way I saw it I didn't have much choice. I had to put my faith in something. Something lime green, or I'd never get out of here.

"Okay, okay, you don't have to light a fire under my sneakers. I'll do it."

Swallowing hard, I walked up to the door, scratched at the bottom, and meowed.

Nothing. I meowed again, louder this time. I heard a grunt from inside and heavy footsteps approaching. I zipped around the side of the bunkhouse, just as the door opened and the guard stuck out his head.

Mistake. Big mistake for him. Madam Yang jumped on his head from on top of the roof, breathing fire at the same time. The man fell flat on his face and dropped his gun. Quickly I kicked it out of his reach.

"No, don't even think about turning around," I said in my deepest voice. "Keep your mouth shut and you won't be hurt." But he'd gotten a good look at Madam Yang and her teeth glittering in the moonlight, and his eyes weren't tracking too well. He gave a groan, whispered, *"¡Chupacabras!"* and *"¡Monstruo!"* before passing out cold.

The dragon looked at me, a question in her eyes.

I was pleased I knew something she didn't. I shrugged. "He probably just thought he saw your basic, normal, blood-sucking, goat-killing, child-stealing kind of monster that roams these parts." I couldn't resist a dig. "A distant cousin of yours, probably."

The dragon blew smoke at me, but didn't say anything.

I retrieved the gun, then threw it as far away as I could. Madam Yang nodded at me approvingly.

Then the dragon put a claw to her lips. "Now go in, and untie Roberto. I'll be near you, but I'm not going to show myself, if I can help it. The fewer people who see me the better. When this guy wakes up, if he has any sense, he'll keep his mouth shut about me and invent a whole gang of rescuers. Don Carlos won't be happy if he thinks his hired gun's been drinking on the job, seeing uh . . . monsters."

I walked through the wall, I mean through the door that wasn't there in my time, and quickly freed Roberto, sawing through the hard knots with my pocket knife. Roberto stood up, rubbed his hands, and asked if Atanacia had sent me.

I nodded. "She's coming soon, I think, out by the corral."

Roberto fished into his vest and pulled out his pocket watch. "We don't have much time, *amigo*. There must be something we can do to slow down anyone sent after us." We stuck the guard facedown on the bed and tied his arms and feet.

All the time, I could see Roberto thinking over the problem, trying to fit the pieces together like it was a jigsaw puzzle, the border in place, but the middle still a mystery. He blew out the lantern's flame and shut the door.

A couple of the horses started whinnying when they saw Roberto, and he reached into his pocket for something to keep them quiet. Then he opened the gate and let them all out, except for the two getaway horses.

"Oh, I get it." I laughed. "Good thinking! You're letting the air out of their tires."

Roberto gave me a funny look as he swatted the last horse on the rump and closed the gate. Atanacia showed up two minutes later, with a dark shawl covering most of her dress. Roberto didn't waste any time (well, there was one quick kiss), cupping his hands to boost Atanacia up onto the smaller horse.

Then he threw me up behind Atanacia. "You can ride, can't you?"

Me? Skateboards are more my style. A little late to be asking that question, I thought as the horse sidestepped nervously and I grabbed handfuls of lace to steady myself. "Uh—"

"Doesn't matter," Roberto said, grinning. "You don't have to do anything but hang on!" He vaulted into his own saddle. Clint Eastwood couldn't have done it better. Atanacia urged her horse on and suddenly we were galloping down the path at a terrific speed. My rear end bounced up and down, never in sync with the horse's. In ten minutes, we were out on the main road, which I somehow recognized though in my time it wore an asphalt topcoat. "Let me off here," I whispered to Atanacia, and when she reined in I slid gracelessly, but gratefully, off the horse.

"Listen," said Atanacia. "You saved me from Eduardo. You saved my life and you rescued Roberto. I cannot thank you enough, and—and, I may never see you again."

"I'm kind of sure of that," I said, tracing a design in the dust with my sneaker toe to hide my embarrassment. "I, uh, I may not get back here for a long, long time myself."

"Listen well. I'm coming back when I'm older to kick my uncle and my greedy coxcomb—he wears more cologne than Napoleon ever did—of a cousin off my hacienda." Atanacia spoke with confidence. "I don't have anything to give you for your trouble now. But I'll bury it at the northeast corner of the hacienda, so you'll know I've succeeded. Look for it when you come back, *sí*?"

"What will I look for?"

"I don't know yet. I'll have to think. But you will know. Good-bye—I don't even know your name. But thank you! *Vaya con Dios*." She blew me a quick kiss, then she was gone.

"*Vaya con Dios,* yourself," I said. "Go with God." A moment later Madam Yang appeared by my side.

"Not bad," she commented. "A knight of the Round Table couldn't have done better or been half as sneaky." Slowly we headed back for the bunkhouse and the fire pit that had started it all.

Natalie was tugging at my shirtsleeve. "Let me try."

"Let you try what?" My eyes were dazzled by the sudden bright light.

"The magic, of course."

"But it already happened."

At first she didn't believe me. Even as I got to the end of my story, she still looked skeptical. As far as she was concerned, I'd just had my hand in a hole with my eyes closed for a minute or two. I knew I could prove it. I knew I was going to have a bruise from Atanacia's horse. But there are limits. Besides, she'd say I got it some other way. Natalie's a logical girl. She puts circuit boards together.

Madam Yang interrupted our wrangling. "Remember, Rick, Atanacia promised to leave you a token. You can look for that. It may still be waiting."

"What are you talking about?" Natalie still had an I-don't-buy-this expression on her face. Quickly I explained.

"Okay," said Natalie. "Get your bike."

Since mine isn't a mountain bike we had to go the long way round, on the main road, then turned off it to the park. Madam Yang trailed us from the air. I noticed the differences from when I'd last been here, ten minutes and who knows how many years ago: blacktop on the roads, handicapped access trails, interpretive signs. We hid our bikes behind some bushes and headed in.

Toward the back the park resembled a construction site, with yellow plastic tape strung up where they didn't want you walking.

A sunburned man, his hair pulled back in a ponytail, perched on a picnic table eating a sandwich. A young woman sat next to him balancing a calculator on her knee. They were deep in discussion. The woman pushed a button, then handed the calculator to her companion. "See, I told you," I heard her say. "Statistically significant."

"This way," said Natalie, and we made like ants and snuck behind them as statistically insignificantly as we could. "Those are archaeologists from the university," Natalie whispered. "They've been surveying the site."

There wasn't a whole lot left of the ranch house. I guess adobe crumbles away eventually, if you don't take care of it. A few partial walls still stood, like chocolate bars left too long in the sun.

"Well?" Natalie had her arms crossed in front of her chest.

"Atanacia said the northeast corner."

We did the limbo under the yellow tape, then crouched down low to the ground so we wouldn't be spotted. At the northeast corner (Natalie had to lead me—I wasn't oriented yet), we stopped. Madam Yang came fluttering down and started digging. Good thing, because the ground was like cement. We couldn't have done it without her claws.

"I think I feel something," she said.

I reached into the hole she'd made and felt something hard. I ran my nails around the edges to loosen the dirt. It was hard work and I wasn't getting anywhere. Then I got the idea to use a stick. With that as leverage, I pried the object from the earth's grasp. I took it out of the hole.

It was the saint's medal Atanacia had worn around her neck. And its container?

A seashell. I had one like it in my collection. Atanacia had made it to California.

Lucky girl.

"—Hey! You kids aren't supposed to be back here! The walls aren't stable." The man and woman from the picnic table came running over. Natalie and I moved away from the wall. Quickly Madam Yang expelled some smoke and disappeared. I felt the breeze on my shins as she slithered by. The man started into a lecture. When he got to the part about the tensile strength of adobe, the woman cut him off.

"What did you find?" she interrupted him. "We have to document it, if it's anything important."

"Just these." I handed over the saint's medal and the seashell. She turned them over, wonderingly.

"This is what you found?" she quizzed me.

"Yeah, in the dirt." I pointed. "Right over there."

"The medal was inside the shell," added Natalie.

"Hmm . . . Well, then I don't think the shell was used for a tool or anything. I guess you can have it back. I'll make a note. The medal's a more recent artifact, something left over from ranch days. This whole area used to be a cattle ranch, but that's not what we're interested in. We're excavating part of a Hohokam Indian settlement—A.D. 700 to 900."

"And you're messing up our dig," added the man. He looked poised to start lecturing again, but Natalie was too quick for him.

"We'll just be on our way," Natalie said brightly. "So sorry for any inconvenience." She walked away with the dignity of the queen of England. I trailed her like a disgraced courtier.

When Madam Yang caught up with us, she observed, "Funny what difference a few centuries make. In another five hundred years or so, they might be interested in Atanacia's medal."

That was fine with me. I got to keep it. I could use a good luck charm.

Chapter 5

The Proper Diet
for a Dragon

"Bad news," said Natalie when I called her the next day, after my mom disappeared into her darkroom. "I've got the shrimp all afternoon. My mother has to take the car in."

"Do you think he'll say anything?"

"Well, Ben's only five. We can't trust him with any state secrets, but my parents are always saying what an active imagination he has," she replied. "I think it'll be okay."

Fifteen minutes later, she and Ben were knocking on my door. Scrawnier than his big sister, Ben wore grubby shorts and a striped T-shirt. In his arms he carried several picture books.

"He never goes anywhere without Dr. Seuss," Natalie informed me as I invited them in. She added, "I told him you had an IGUANA. He wants to see it."

I led the way to my room. Madam Yang lounged on the bed, reading my mom's *Vogue*. She was probably imagining how the supermodels would taste. The dragon held a marshmallow impaled on her right claw. We watched as she breathed lightly on it, then a little harder, toasting it to a perfect golden brown. She popped it in her mouth.

"I want one!" said Ben.

"You can't have an iguana, Ben," said Natalie. "You're not old enough for a pet."

"I want a marshmallow!" Ben persisted.

Madam Yang asked for and received a proper introduction, before whipping out a marshmallow for Ben. The Jet Puff bag was already half empty. Mom had been on my case that morning about food disappearing. She was wondering why I couldn't eat some snacks at Natalie's house. I told her Natalie's parents were into healthy food in a big way and all they had in their fridge was carrot sticks and tofu. She didn't believe me, but let it pass.

"No offense," I told the dragon, "but if you eat too many of those, you'll get sick. I know from experience."

The dragon ignited Ben's marshmallow, then waved it in the air to put out the flame.

"See what you made me do," she said, moving her ears back in irritation. "I'll have you know I have a cast-iron stomach. We won't even talk about experience."

It's foolish to argue with a dragon.

"I like them that way," put in Ben. "That's the way I always make them."

Madam Yang smiled and handed over the char-coaled marshmallow.

"Would you read me a story?" asked Ben. "Please?"

Madam Yang nodded. "True education begins with books, my young knight errant. You are wise beyond your years to recognize that." Ben climbed up on the bed and snuggled next to her. He handed her a book. As Natalie and I left the room, we heard the dragon ask Ben to turn the pages. Two-inch nails aren't real practical, I guess.

Natalie looked at me. "How are you handling it?"

The strain must be showing. Mom had checked my temp that morning, but you don't run a fever when your disease is a combination of homesickness and dragonitis. I'd dodged her questions, but she had that look in her eyes: I'm-worried-and-I'm-going-to-get-to-the-bottom-of-this. The dragon wouldn't be a long-term secret if food kept disappearing.

"Well, so far, I've managed to keep Madam Yang under wraps," I told Natalie. "She sleeps in my closet, says it reminds her of a cave, but she made me move my sneakers out. And she snores, though she says she doesn't. Mom doesn't come in my room without asking, so that part's all right. And in this heat, I don't think Mom's going to be calling Dragonwerks asking what happened to the furnace any time soon." We had moved the crate out behind some bushes in the backyard and pulled all the labels off, so Mom wouldn't see it and wonder. "But Madam Yang keeps eating, you know? And I don't know what I'll do once school starts."

"I can sneak over some food, if that would help," Natalie offered.

"Thanks. It would."

Then Natalie said she wanted to see my mom's pictures, so I showed her some, and we got out the photo album, too, and pretty soon I was showing her the snaps of me, starting with gooey, drooling baby. I would have flipped past those, but Natalie stopped me.

"That's your dad?" she asked, pointing at the dark-haired man in whose lap I sat. My baby self had a tight grip on both his thumbs.

"Yeah," I said. "He died before I turned two. I don't really remember him." Just that I liked to be swung high in the air, but I'm too big for that now. I turned the page to get away from the memory. Natalie didn't ask any more questions about him. I pointed to the next set of photos.

"See, here's where we lived in San Diego. My friend Santiago lived next door. Here he is. We bought a skateboard together last summer—neither of us had enough money to get a good one on his own, so we took turns using it."

"What did you do with it?"

I shrugged. "There aren't any sidewalks here. I left it with him."

"I think you just might be a good friend to have, Rick Morales."

I think my ears turned red. Looking at Santiago's grin, I remembered I hadn't written him, not even a postcard to say I'm here, you're not, and it's mega-hot. We'd had a big argument the day before I left—probably because I was leaving. It was either that or cry, and we were too macho to do that. Funnily enough, the argument started over missing persons: our dads. Santiago's parents were divorced and he hadn't seen his dad in over two years. When he said that was worse than me, that I didn't even remember enough about my father to be sad, I saw red.

Even if it were true, it's like the difference between getting your kite stuck in a tree and having it disappear into the ozone, I told Santiago. You might get your kite back, but I can't. There's this hole over my head all the time, even if you can't see it. It's there. In the ozone, *mi amigo*? Santiago asked. Then he told me I had a hole in my head. That's when I slugged him.

Still, it wasn't an argument either of us could win—we were evenly matched—but I have to point out, at least Santiago's dad called him on his birthday. Since my *abuela* Josefina died, I hadn't had anyone to talk to about my dad. It still makes my mom sad, so I don't bring him up much.

Now, talking to Natalie, I thought I should send Santiago a postcard and ask if he'd mastered any new skateboard moves.

An hour later into Monopoly, I owned Boardwalk and Park Place, and jail was all Natalie could hope for. I was about to throw the dice when Ben came rushing out. "Nat, Madam Yang is sick," he said. The three of us ran back to my room. Madam Yang's eyes were closed and she had both front legs clutched to her stomach, her head dangling off the foot of the bed. She moaned. Her forehead felt chilly. The empty marshmallow bag squished between my toes.

"Madam Yang?"

She groaned.

"You don't feel so good?"

Another, more emphatic groan. She burped, and a small fireball shot out of her mouth. It landed on the carpet right in front of me, singeing the hair on my legs. I jumped back, then stamped out the flame before it could do any real damage. It smelled like toasted marshmallows in there in a major way. Madam Yang started panting, puffs of smoke coming out in short bursts.

"Hang on, Madam Yang," I said. "We'll get you some help."

Natalie said there was a pet clinic down by the library. "Let's try the library first, though."

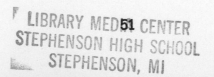

"Yeah," I agreed. "It's not a good idea to give people heart attacks."

"Good thing I brought Ben," she added. "We can take Madam Yang in his bike trailer. Oh, I hope she's okay!"

Moving fast, I rounded up my shoes from under my bed. I knocked on the darkroom door—hard—to tell Mom we were going out. Then Natalie and I wrapped Madam Yang in a blanket, cocooning her in warmth. Her eyes glowed dull red, glazed. We shuffled her outside and stowed her in the red-and-yellow trailer. Madam Yang weighed less than expected, but there still wasn't room for Ben; he'd have to ride on my handlebars. Luckily he was a lightweight and knew enough not to wiggle. We rode slowly, sticking to side roads until we reached Puma Canyon Plaza. We parked the bikes under a tree and left Ben on guard duty.

Marcella Mortenson looked up, but we rushed right over to a computer terminal.

"Type *S* for subject," Natalie directed.

"We already looked up dragons," I argued. "We got all those books on folklore. We need something useful."

"Well, maybe something about lizards, then."

"Madam Yang's not a lizard!"

"But she's reptilian, don't you think?"

"May I help you?" Marcella hovered over us. Our voices went down to whisper level.

I recovered first. "Uh, we're working on a project."

"School's not in session, is it?"

"It's not exactly for school. Could you help us?"

"I suppose it's due tomorrow." It was not a question.

"As soon as possible, only, we're having trouble finding out information."

"Let's try a keyword search. It can link information for you. May I?" I surrendered my chair to her. "What is it you want to know?"

"Uh, stuff about indigestion, symptoms of appendicitis, pet care for, uh, dragons."

The librarian stopped typing and her eyebrows shot up. "Did you say 'dragons'?"

"Like a really, really big lizard," said Natalie.

"Godzilla," said Marcella.

"No, not that big," said Natalie hastily. "Like the size of a big dog."

"Shaped like a burrito," I added.

Marcella was cool. She didn't ask any more questions, just typed. The keyword search yielded two possibilities, but one was checked out. The other was titled *Raising Dragons: The Complete Care Guide*.

"There's a copy at the main library," Marcella informed us. "Shall I order it? It will take a few days to get here."

"Thanks, there's not enough time," I told her.

"Maybe your mother can drive you down, then." Right, with a dragon throwing up in the backseat. We thanked the librarian for trying.

"I'll put a hold on it anyway. Then no one else can check it out if you two change your minds."

Outside, we looked at each other.

"Now what?" asked Natalie.

I pointed at the pet clinic across the parking lot. "We'll have to risk it. Grab the bikes."

We took Madam Yang inside. Ben carried her tail to keep it from dragging. She wasn't moving.

The vet's waiting room smelled a little doggy, but was empty, thank goodness. The receptionist looked up.

"Can I help you?"

"My pet's sick," I said. "Can the vet see her?"

"That's what he's here for. Have you been in before?" she asked.

"No, but my mom brought in our cat at the beginning of the week." She made me fill out a piece of paper. I wrote down "Komodo dragon," and crossed my fingers the vet hadn't seen one, since I was sure he hadn't seen anything like Madam Yang before. I got stuck at the blanks for my address and phone number. "I just moved here," I explained, "but I know my mom was in here a few days ago."

"What's the name?" the receptionist asked.

"Morales."

"And the pet's name? The one your mom brought in?"

"Fat Boy."

"Okay, I'll photocopy his data sheet and stick it in the new chart."

"Thanks," I said.

When she had finished, the receptionist led us into the examination room. We waited till the door closed behind her before unwrapping Madam Yang. If anything, the dragon looked worse. Her eyes were still closed and she had turned a funny color, a sort of sickly pale green. She'd shed several scales and they stuck to the blanket.

There came a knock on the door and the vet stepped briskly into the room. Tall and on the thin side, at first he seemed to have eyes only for me. Pointing to the chart, he asked, "You're Sylvia Morales's son? You just moved here from San Diego?" When I nodded, he went on, "I'm Evan Cotter. It's nice to meet you. I had such a good conversation with your mother the other day." He hesitated for a second, then asked, "Is it just the two of you?" I said it was. He looked like he wanted to ask more questions, but I pointed toward Madam Yang and he got down to business.

"What have we here, eh?"

We moved aside to let Dr. Cotter see Madam Yang. She slumped forward, her nose resting on her forelegs. Only a thin wisp of smoke issued from her nostrils.

The vet had started to step forward, but quickly swung his leg backward, as if he were a marionette whose puppeteer had changed his mind. Finally he put his leg down. Without moving any closer, he asked, "Is that some kind of crocodile?"

"No, she's a very rare reptile. My uncle collects them down in South America." I crossed two fingers behind my back.

Dr. Cotter consulted the chart again. "A Komodo dragon from South America. Funny, I thought they came from Indonesia." He hadn't moved any closer.

"Well, she's originally from Indonesia," I invented. "When my uncle took her to South America, er—"

"To Paraguay," added Natalie helpfully.

"Yes, to what she said, and my uncle found he couldn't keep her, he sent her to me."

"Rather than a zoo."

"Right." I needed more fingers at the rate I was fibbing. "Uh, please don't say anything to my mom about her. I haven't had Madam Yang long, and I want to pick the right time to tell her."

"Does she, uh, bite?"

"She's quite tame," said Natalie, trying to move the conversation forward, "and she really needs your help. Like right now," she added.

The vet approached gingerly and put his hand on the dragon's neck. Madam Yang moaned softly, but didn't move. He took out a thermometer but thought better of it and stuck it back in the drawer unused. Then his professional manner took over and he quickly examined Madam Yang from stem to stern, finishing by palpating her abdomen.

"I think I know what's causing the distress," he said. "Could you tell me what you've been feeding your pet?"

"Well, she's mostly been eating peanut butter and jelly sandwiches. But she had toasted marshmallows this morning; I'm not really sure how many."

"Twenty-six," put in Ben. "I counted."

Dr. Cotter shook his head. "No wonder she's sick. You'd get sick, too, if that's what you ate."

"Well, I did try to warn her—" Dr. Cotter was looking at me strangely. Hastily, I added, "I'll put the marshmallows where she can't get at them."

"I've never had experience with this kind of, uh, exotic pet." He hesitated on the last word. "But, I think the best thing would be to try a liquid diet for a day or two—"

"You mean like Gatorade, apple juice?"

"No, plain old water is best. You're looking to prevent dehydration," Dr. Cotter explained. "Then, in twenty-four hours, if she's doing well—crickets are the ticket."

"Bugs?"

"Best thing for her. You can buy them live at any pet store. Later, rats and mice, when she's ready to hunt. Stay away from sweets, of course." He scribbled something in the chart.

Madam Yang moaned faintly and rasped, "Oh, for a good princess. That would settle my stomach."

Dr. Cotter turned around. "Did you say something?" Natalie and I shook our heads.

But Ben almost gave away the game. "She did!" he said, pointing at Madam Yang. "She said something."

Natalie put her hand over his mouth. "You know how little kids are," she said, standing tall to look grown up.

Ben pulled her hand away and glared at his sister. "She did *too* say something, Gnat-girl! She said—"

Madam Yang cleared her throat, interrupting Ben. It sounded like a giraffe gargling and it took a long time. Ben shut up.

Dr. Cotter stood there, not knowing what to think. His eyes narrowed as he looked from me to Natalie to Ben, then again at Madam Yang. "Okay, the best thing would be to take your, er, Komodo dragon home and let her rest," he finally said. "You can call me if there are any further problems. Let me know how she does. Oh, and do you want me to talk to your mother about her? I've got a pretty good track record with stray kittens and dogs—"

"That's okay," I hastened to assure him. "This is different." The look in his eyes showed me he agreed. I continued, "I'll tell her myself. When it looks like the right time. You don't see a pet like this every day."

"No," said Dr. Cotter. "Certainly you don't. I'd say she's unique." He helped us wrap Madam Yang up again and carried her out to the bike trailer himself through the side door, so we didn't have to go through the waiting room.

"I'll check on her later," the vet called to us. He waved as we pedaled off.

When we reached home, I confirmed that my mom was still a million miles away in her dark-room, then Natalie and I hustled Madam Yang into my room. In the kitchen I filled a cup with water.

Madam Yang sipped a little, then thanked me. Before I could untangle the cup from her claws, she was snoring.

"Exhibit A," I said, pointing. "A dragon that doesn't snore. You're my witnesses."

Chapter 6

The Dragon's Lair

"Evan Cotter's asked us out for pizza tonight," my mom announced over Cheerios at breakfast. She looked real pleased, like Fat Boy when he sees me getting out the can opener.

"Who's that?" I played dumb, as if I hadn't seen his business card stuck on the wall by the phone. As if I hadn't been in his waiting room recently.

"You know, the vet. He's nice." Mom didn't add she thought I'd like him. She'd learned not to overdo.

"I'm too old for a sitter, so don't even think about it." I crossed my arms in front of my chest.

"You're invited, too. We're family, remember?"

I don't know many families where one person decides they're moving four hundred miles away without asking anyone else's opinion.

"Yes, ma'am." I saluted.

Mom narrowed her eyes and crossed her arms in front of her chest. She looked a lot like Madam Yang at her most irritated. Then Mom changed gears and asked me about my plans for the day. I knew Natalie wanted to go adventuring with the dragon—hopefully following a nice safe peanut butter scent trail—but I couldn't tell Mom that. So I just said maybe we'd go swimming at Natalie's. Mom said she'd be back in the early afternoon. She told me to be back by five, to clean up. I knew not to be late.

You'd think it would be hard to conceal a dragon walking down the road in broad daylight. But this was Tucson, not San Diego. The houses are set far apart, on a little over three acres, in this part of town. And not many cars roll down the road. If one does, you can hear it way before you see it. Plenty of time for a green dragon to melt into the scrubby bushes edging the park.

Within a few minutes, Madam Yang and I arrived at Natalie's back door. "It's okay," she said. "Coast's clear. Mom took Ben shopping for shoes and his first set of school clothes. He can't wait to be in kindergarten. They'll be at it for a while." We headed for Natalie's room, where Madam Yang flopped down in a beanbag. I sat in the desk chair and Natalie perched on the end of her bed, swinging her feet impatiently.

She'd been arguing for days that she deserved a turn going back in time, but Madam Yang seemed reluctant.

Now the dragon cautioned, "I'm good at booking crises. They're easy to sniff out, just like peeling back the layers of an onion: Time is more pungent at certain points. But, you know, it does take a lot of energy to go back and forth through time. And there are no guarantees of safety." Madam Yang had practically slept around the clock after the Atanacia adventure. She still looked peaked from the marshmallow incident, although most of her color had returned. If she had cold feet, that was okay with me. Curious I might be, but not stupid.

"Yeah, Natalie," I added, "Madam Yang's right. Those were real bullets they fired a hundred-odd years ago. Getting hurt is possible. And getting out might not be."

"Then can't we go somewhere, even if it's not back in time?" Natalie doesn't know when to give up.

The dragon looked at Natalie from under hooded lids. "Do you want to try something else because you're dying for your own adventure or because you're not convinced that Rick here didn't play an elaborate trick on you?"

"Both," said Natalie brazenly. She always blurted out the truth.

I was surprised then, when the dragon grinned back at her, a scary sight involving many pointed teeth.

"Truthfulness is rarely found, and the more prized for being rare." The dragon paused to think. "I suppose . . . Hmm . . . Well, maybe we could tilt time on its axis and shift the venue instead."

"Huh?" I said.

"I know a safe place and time," Madam Yang explained. "That is . . . give or take a century."

I hummed the theme from *The Twilight Zone*. Natalie narrowed her eyes at me.

"This is my adventure. You just keep quiet and follow," said Natalie. "That is if you don't want to get left behind." She stood up and grabbed her backpack.

"Oh, but, we don't have to go anywhere," said the dragon. "Just sit down, relax, and try to concentrate on nothing. Let me do the work. Closing your eyes might help. Of course, you need to be touching me."

Reassured that it wouldn't be like the first time—when my desire to be back in California collided with Atanacia's and dumped me in the past—I forgot to be scared. I grabbed hold of one of the soft supple ridges marching down Madam Yang's back and Natalie copied me.

Have you ever tried to make your mind a blank? If you do, you'll find it's almost impossible. I decided to concentrate on the ocean on a calm day, out past the breakers, just lazy green swells rising and falling. Bit by bit I erased the sailboats, then the dolphins. The screaming seagulls were the last to go.

I shifted in my seat. The carpet felt lumpy, damp, and hard. In fact, it didn't feel like carpet at all. I opened my eyes and couldn't see anything. It was totally dark. With my free hand, I felt around me. It was hard and cold. We were definitely not in Natalie's room anymore.

"Madam Yang?"

"Just let me get my bearings. I haven't been here in a while. Actually decades."

"Madam Yang!"

Natalie snapped on her flashlight. Once the dazzle left my eyes, I could see we were in a cave tunnel, tons of grayish rock, with threads of darker charcoal running through it. It smelled musty. Bats? I stood up. My head bumped against the ceiling. "Ouch!" echoed for a long time.

"Madam Yang, where is this place?"

"It's my lair, actually," she answered. She inhaled deeply, held her breath for a few seconds, then exhaled steam. "Ah, it feels good to be home." Then she turned and beckoned. "Follow me. We have to descend another one hundred feet or so."

Madam Yang led the way, blowing fire ahead, both to supplement the beam of Natalie's flashlight and warm the decidedly damp and chilly air. Still, it felt like I was getting goose bumps on top of goose bumps. Before long we emerged from the tunnel into a good-size cavern. Madam Yang vanished behind a boulder and returned holding a lantern, which she proceeded to light. Natalie switched off her flashlight to save the batteries.

"Just sit tight and I'll have a fire going in no time." Madam Yang shuffled around, looking behind and under a few rocks, but came back empty clawed.

"Looks like I'll have to run out for some firewood. I'll be back soon!"

She squeezed into an opening at the cavern's far end and disappeared.

"Some adventure," I remarked, jumping up and down for warmth. As a hostess, Madam Yang could do with some handy homemaking tips. Natalie had switched her flashlight back on and was peering into crevices.

"Look, there's some clothing over here," she said, tossing me a bundle. "Put it on; we don't know how long she'll be gone."

Unrolled, the bundle proved to be a dress, long and velvety with fur trim around the neck and wrists. I had no choice. It was either the dress or hypothermia. If I'd been where anybody from school could see me, I'd have chosen hypothermia. It would have been a quicker, kinder death. Quickly

I pulled the dress on over my T-shirt and shorts. I warned Natalie that if she ever told anyone about this, I'd have her head.

"Who'd believe me?" she shot back. When she emerged from behind her changing boulder, she wore a long dark robe with stars and moons embroidered on it. They twinkled in the lantern light. There was a long pointed cap to match.

"Hey, we should trade," I said. "That's a wizard's costume."

"So?"

"Well, wizards are, like, guys."

"So?"

"Like me!"

In the middle of our argument we heard a sound like chalk scraping on a blackboard. It was coming from the tunnel Madam Yang had left by, but the steps were heavier and the smell was different, sharper. First we saw a tail, and then the back end of a dragon go past the opening. Only this dragon was quite a bit plumper than Madam Yang. The creature exhaled, and with effort, squeezed into the cavern. Natalie disappeared around the boulder. Hampered by my long skirts, I couldn't run.

The dragon turned around and I froze. He—I knew it was a he from the Fu Manchu mustache—was evidently a throwback to an earlier age. If Madam Yang was collie size, this dragon rivaled a St. Bernard and probably ate collies. He had eyes as big as pie tins and they widened when they caught sight of me. He smiled, but it wasn't friendly.

"Dinnertime!" he said. "My favorite meal of princess delivered right to my door. How serendipitous!" The dragon came closer and sniffed at my skirts.

"No perfume," he said regretfully. "Oh, well, can't have everything." He opened a mouth full of teeth and I found myself staring down his gullet past his tonsils to the black hole beyond. I swear I could feel its gravitational pull.

"Wait a sec. You're making a big mistake," I stammered.

"Oh?" said the dragon, bored with my feeble effort to avoid being eaten. But his eyes lit up as Natalie popped out from behind the boulder. She advanced on the dragon, swishing a wand in front of his nose.

"You can't eat him." Her voice didn't shake and the echo helped. I noticed she stood very straight, trying to look taller.

"Him?"

"Yes, he's a boy, you dim-witted reptile. I'm the real princess. We switched clothes, you know, so I could be incognita? It's such a bother going out into the countryside, everyone asking you for your autograph. You don't know how it is. You'll have to eat me, Lizard-breath, if you're going to eat anyone. But you're not going to because I have magic powers and I'll use them if I have to!"

"Mm," said the dragon, unimpressed. "Dinner and dessert." He opened his mouth, ready to take a chunk out of my leg. My life should have been flashing in front of my eyes, but all I could see were those teeth. I jumped back and grabbed for a cantaloupe-size rock.

At the same time, Natalie brought down the wand with a crack on the dragon's nose.

Chapter 7

Some Enchantments
Are Better Left That Way

Sparks flew, and a crack like thunder echoed for a long time.

When I opened my eyes, the dragon had disappeared. In his place squatted a small green frog. I snatched him up before he could hop away. He tried to squirm out of my grasp and I squeezed hard, then stowed him in my pocket.

We heard scrabbling in the tunnel again. Madam Yang came puffing into view, carrying a load of firewood. She set it down and lit the kindling before we could tell her what had happened. Quickly she had a cheerful fire going. It made a big difference in the cave atmosphere, I can tell you. The musty smell vaporized, replaced by clean burning pine.

"I hope I wasn't gone too long," she apologized. "It took me a while to find dry wood. Everything's wet out there."

"Uh, Madam Yang?"

"Yes, Rick?"

"Someone else, some other dragon, has taken over your lair."

"A squatter? You're not serious?" She could see by our faces that we were. Then she noticed our clothes.

"There are bones, too," Natalie said. She hadn't told me that. What did she think I was, squeamish? Yes, ma'am. The dress suddenly felt tight. I didn't want to think about what had happened to its owner.

Madam Yang still looked skeptical.

Quickly we explained about the other dragon. Madam Yang's eyes grew wide. When we got to the part where I would have been eaten if Natalie hadn't intervened, Madam Yang sat down hard on the floor. Natalie showed her the wizard's wand. Madam Yang turned it over in her talons.

"It shouldn't have worked, you know," she told Natalie. "You're not trained. And besides, wizardry is still a sexist profession. I wonder . . ." She thought some more. "Yes, I see, the wizard must have said the spell, but been ah—"

"Eaten," put in Natalie.

"That's right, consumed before he could complete the passes." Madam Yang sniffed. "Personally, I never eat wizards. All that hair, and gristle? Ugh. However, each to his own taste. My dear, you got lucky."

I lifted up my skirt and fished the frog out of my pocket, holding him out for inspection.

"So, here he is. What's left of him."

"Ah," said Madam Yang. "This is someone I don't recognize."

"Of course you don't," the frog piped up. "I don't usually look this way."

Madam Yang glared at the amphibian and he quit talking. She took him from me and examined him carefully. "Well, we can't leave him this way. It's unnatural."

Privately, I thought we jolly well could. I mean, how much trouble could he cause as a frog? Bugs might live in fear, but people wouldn't. Nat evidently agreed and we argued with Madam Yang, but she wouldn't have any of it. We had messed around with magic—true, in a good cause and in an emergency dial 9-1-1 situation—but we would have to fix it. You couldn't leave magic halfway. It was Against the Rules.

Natalie pointed out that if the frog turned back into a dragon, we would be back in danger. "He's big, Madam Yang."

I described his teeth in detail.

Madam Yang swished her tail dismissively. "There is only one thing to do. No, it doesn't involve the wizard's wand. That can be dangerous in the wrong hands." Then she told us her plan.

"You're kidding," I said.

"No way," gasped Natalie. "No possible way am I kissing that thing!"

"I'm not a thing," peeped the frog indignantly.

"And I'm not a princess!" said Natalie, just as mad. "I tell you, it won't work!"

Madam Yang soothed her and said it should work. "Really, the princess thing is overexaggerated. The kiss just has to be willingly given. Any girl can kiss a frog. Many do."

Then Madam Yang made the frog promise not to eat us. I didn't quite trust him, but Madam Yang knew what she was doing.

The frog hopped onto Natalie's palm. She shivered at his touch. She brought him close to her face, looked into his bulgy eyes, and shuddered. But gamely she closed her own and puckered up. The frog launched himself toward her lips, as if Natalie couldn't be trusted not to change her mind.

Again lightning flashed and thunder crashed. When our eyes and ears had recovered, we saw a decidedly confused young man standing in front of us. He wore moldy silk stockings and striped pantaloons topped with an embroidered vest over a shirt with lots of lace dripping from the collar and cuffs. A crown perched on brown curls completed his ensemble. He dropped to his satin knees and would have kissed the toes of Natalie's high tops if she hadn't edged backward.

"Oh, thank you for releasing me. I've been under an enchantment for so long."

"This is your real form?" asked Madam Yang. She looked dazed.

"Yes, Prince Rupert at your service." He jumped up and hugged himself and started doing a dance. Then he stopped and looked at Natalie. Her hair had fallen out of its ponytail and fell around her shoulders, glowing brightly in the firelight. She looked almost pretty. Rupert must have thought so, too, because he suddenly became tongue-tied. He occupied himself pushing a stone with his toe, then finally addressed her. "You know, it's somewhat traditional that the one who breaks the spell gets to marry me."

"And just what is that supposed to mean? After you almost eat me, you want to marry me?" Natalie poked Rupert, the frog prince, in the chest to emphasize her point. "You have got to be kidding. There is no way!"

Madam Yang quickly stepped between the two of them. "Rules, like spells, are made to be broken," she said grimly. "Natalie doesn't belong here, nor do you, Rupert, so, here, take this lantern, and go."

Rupert did, after lots more bowing. "My castle's just over the hill. My parents will be so glad to see me." He practically skipped out the tunnel.

"I'm a little worried," said Madam Yang. "About the future . . . You know, once you develop a taste for princesses, it stays with you. I fear for Rupert's future bride." She shook her head.

"Well, children, are you ready to go back?"

She didn't have to ask. We peeled off the borrowed clothes, glommed onto our dragon, and closed our eyes. In a moment, we were back in Natalie's room, blinking our eyes in the sudden brightness. I looked at Natalie. Bravery isn't limited to grizzled men defending the ramparts. I touched her arm. She jumped.

"Natalie?"

"Mm?"

"Just thanks."

"You're welcome," she said. She smiled at me.

Madam Yang had slipped into her fussbudget role. "I'm going to have to report this, you know. And my superiors aren't going to like it one bit. Definitely not part of the assignment."

"What superiors? What assignment?" I dared to ask her.

"If I told you, I'd be in even more trouble. That would risk gumming up the whole works." Still, she relented a bit. "Someday maybe," she promised. I would have to be content with that.

With the dragon muttering about paperwork, we went home.

*   *   *

Dr. Cotter picked us up in his car. Mom introduced us and he played along with it, pretending he hadn't met me before. That impressed me, and Mom had no clue whatsoever. As Mom got in front, Dr. Cotter opened the back door for me. He winked at me and said he'd vacuumed up all the dog fur in my honor. It looked like he'd washed and waxed the car, too. I could see my face in the finish. The backseat smelled a little doggy, but not too bad.

We had thick, gooey pizza with a chewy crust. Dr. Cotter, but he said to call him Evan, thought it was the best in Tucson. I had an uncomfortable moment when he asked me how my pet was doing, but I recovered quickly. I said Fat Boy was doing just fine. Very fine, I emphasized, adjusting well. He'd quit spraying the drapes. The vet seemed to understand and dropped the subject. He and Mom got to comparing and contrasting Tucson with San Diego. Even Mom had to admit the weather hadn't been a change for the better.

She laughed when Dr. Cotter managed to say with a straight face, "But it's a dry heat." But even he couldn't hold it in, and burst out laughing. Then Mom got serious.

"Do you know how many drive-by shootings San Diego had last year?" she asked. "I didn't want to get numb. I made up my mind to leave right after prom season, one of my busiest times. There was a girl shot riding home on the school bus. I ended up photographing her in her prom dress, one arm in a sling. And, you know, I thought, it's just a matter of time, before I end up taking pictures of someone in a wheelchair, or worse. . . ."

Mom had no small talk, but Dr. Cotter, I mean Evan, didn't seem to mind. He started telling her about how therapeutic owning an animal can be for troubled kids.

Mom hadn't told me about the girl at the prom before. If she had, maybe I would have understood the move better. Lots of times grown-ups don't think kids should hear frightening things. They want to protect us, but they don't give us enough credit.

Still, it would have been nice to have been asked about the move. Mom's executive decision had changed our world. Once we got home I didn't go to sleep for a long time. Madam Yang snored softly from the closet, but it wasn't that.

I had a lot to think about.

Chapter 8

Dragon Flight

"It's a cinch," Natalie was saying. "Put a leash on her and people won't look twice. You know, they see what they want to see." She paused for dramatic effect. "And what they'll see is the *ugliest* pet in the entire universe!"

Madam Yang glared at Natalie, but her enthusiasm was catching. We had this problem, see, the vet bill, after a certain dragon overdid it with Jet Puff marshmallows. Natalie had practically flown over to my house this morning when she heard about the contest on the radio. KROK would give away fifty dollars to the owner of "the ugliest pet in Tucson." They were sponsoring the competition in honor of the dog days of summer.

We were all sitting at the kitchen table, mulling it over, sharing a round of root beer with lots of ice. Natalie's face was still bright pink from the ride over. Mom had gone out schmoozing—that's what she called it anyway—it meant she was dropping by a couple of the resorts again. She had to make sure the catering managers remembered her face and name, so that they would suggest her to couples coming in to plan their wedding details. Her business was starting to grow, but we were still living off savings: definitely no time to tell her about a vet bill for a dragon she didn't know we had.

"Madam Yang, please say you'll do it," I pleaded. "Then we can pay Dr. Cotter and even have some left over."

"Take that big hair ball you call a pet instead."

"Fat Boy's not a hair ball," I protested. "He's just an overly large, fluffy kitty. And he's not ugly."

"Easily fixed. He'd look ugly if I singed off his fur."

"That is not a good idea, Madam Yang." I wasn't sure she was teasing. "You leave him alone!"

The dragon grumbled. First she wanted to find a pirate and rob his treasure chest, but we had to tell her that pirates weren't so easy to find nowadays even if she could slip in and out of time. No pirate had ever plied the arroyos around Tucson, anyway. Then she told us of a cave filled with treasure, sort of a family inheritance, but it was somewhere in Cornwall, and she admitted she might not know the landmarks by now.

So we tried flattery. We told Madam Yang that we, personally, did not think she was ugly, just unusual. Yeah, she had that rare, unique kind of unusual beauty that lots of people wouldn't identify with, but would make her stand out in any contest. Pleeease?

Eventually she gave in. What part guilt played in her decision, who knows, but certainly she knew she'd blown it on our last adventure. Without Natalie's quick thinking and a lot of luck, I would have been history.

"Where is this contest being held, anyway?" I asked Natalie.

"It's down at Park Mall, in the Center Court, at two o'clock." Natalie checked her watch. "That's one hour and forty-two minutes from now. We can ride our bikes to the bus stop, then catch SunTran into town."

"No way," said Madam Yang. She was picking up our slang. She slurped up the last of her root beer and looked at me to see if I might offer her another. Yeah, right. She added, "I'm not riding in that contraption again," referring to the bike trailer. She associated it with her bout of sickness, but just to be sure, I had hidden the marshmallows.

I tried reasoning with Madam Yang. "Then how will we get there? We need that money. Dr. Cotter will send my mom a bill at the end of the week. The receptionist said so!"

"As usual, you are overlooking the obvious," said the dragon, blowing smoke puffs at the ceiling.

"Stop that," I said. "You'll set off the fire alarm again."

Natalie looked at me, her eyes shining. "I know! I know! We're going to fly!"

"Not both of you," said Madam Yang. "One of you will have to take the bus. I can only handle one of you in my claws."

Claws? Natalie's excitement went into hiding. Obviously she'd pictured herself on the dragon's back, not dangling beneath her like prey. Natalie suggested me since I didn't know where the bus stop or the mall was. Before I knew it, it was settled. The dragon and I would tail the bus.

"I'll meet you at the Center Court just before the contest starts," said Natalie. "Is this going to be good or what? I can't wait!" She sped out of there, not giving Madam Yang a chance to singe her sneakers.

I would like to report that flying by dragon was a wonderful experience, easily the most exciting in my life. Terrifying, yes. Like nothing I'd done before, ditto. Something to be repeated? Well . . . Madam Yang grabbed my shirt with her front claws and lurched forward and up, like a helicopter. Then she snagged my shorts by the back pockets with her hind feet. I prayed they wouldn't rip. I swayed from side to side as she flew, but that wasn't why I felt sick. I mean, I've ridden all the roller coasters at Disneyland before, *no problema*.

It was Madam Yang's breath. She was breathing hard from the exertion and I would bet she hadn't used a toothbrush in easily two centuries, if ever. I plugged my nose, and after that it got easier. We had to circle while Natalie waited for the bus. Once she got on, it was easy to follow it. With my nose plugged, my stomach settled down some and I looked around with interest. All the cars were matchbox size. Nobody looked up and saw us, We didn't stop traffic or cause an accident. After about fifteen minutes, the bus stopped at the mall and Madam Yang hovered while we watched antlike Natalie get out and go in the main entrance. We flew around to a side entrance, where there wasn't as much chance of being seen. We followed a little girl with a tortoiseshell guinea pig in her arms. It had so much hair you couldn't tell the front end from the back.

People gave us, or at least my green friend, a wide berth. One wise guy joked, "Where'd you get your iguana, a nuclear test site?" Ha ha. He's lucky to be alive.

Center Court wasn't hard to find. It resembled a zoo with the animals set free. There were lots of kids with dogs and a few with unhappy cats. I saw a toad, a turtle, one rabbit, and two goats. A couple of adults had pets, too.

Natalie ran up to us. "I've been scoping out the competition," she hissed in my ear. "There's a French poodle with a bad haircut and a fat Rottweiler, but I don't think they've got a chance against Madam Yang."

Madam Yang has very good hearing, I've noticed. She snorted, but remembered to control the smoke, and turned it into a sneeze.

A woman with a megaphone was standing in the middle of Center Court. She asked us all to form a circle, so the judges could walk around.

Madam Yang and I stood in front of a plastic tree with green silk leaves. They weren't itty-bitty leaves, like all the other Tucson trees had. I guess it was supposed to be a shopping oasis in the desert. A kid with a Tamagotchi waited on our left. Pretty pathetic if you ask me, but it's true those virtual pets do get ugly if you forget to discipline them. On my right, a kid was coaching his frog to croak on command.

Then I saw him. He was only half the size of my dragon, but he looked like walking roadkill. All the fur on this dog's rear end was missing. Where the fur should have been was skin the color of boiled ham. His tongue hung like stretched-out bubblegum halfway down his forelegs.

I nudged Natalie. "The competition just heated up."

"Oh, no," she groaned.

Madam Yang's ears perked up and she looked over at the late arrival. Once she'd agreed to do this, she'd decided to win. Dragons are very competitive. "He's toast," she said, and started to inhale. I smelled brimstone in the air, at least that's what I think it was. If you've ever smelled it, it's unmistakable, like rotten eggs but worse.

"Don't you dare," I told her. "You don't think the judge wouldn't notice? I'm sure you're automatically disqualified if you take out a rival."

"What if I just make him disappear? Blow a little smoke his way?"

"The mall is no smoking. Now, be quiet, before someone hears you talking."

Roadkill began scratching himself nonchalantly. The judges finished with him and started heading our way. One was a man dressed in shorts and a T-shirt with KROK on the front. The other was a young woman with a clipboard, taking notes.

Finally it was our turn. "Think ugly," said Natalie.

"Yeah, think St. George," I said, getting a sudden inspiration.

I'm not sure that was the right thing to say, in retrospect. Madam Yang bared all her teeth and made her eyes into little slits. She squatted down like a spider. The ridges on her back bristled. I think she frightened the judges away—they didn't spend a lot of time with us.

Soon they were ready to announce the results. Poodle with a Mohawk, inappropriately named Duchess, took third.

"Imitation royalty," Madam Yang sniffed. I shushed her.

Then the man said he was going to ask the two ugliest pets to come up and get everyone in the audience to help him decide. He called out my name and that of Roadkill's owner.

Natalie was jumping up and down, her ponytail bouncing with her. "Yes, yes!"

Slowly Madam Yang and I walked to the center. Roadkill and his owner did, too. Roadkill's owner was dressed in black with a safety pin stuck in his nose and a tattoo of a cobra on his right biceps. Good thing Roadkill's owner couldn't enter—he would have won hands down.

Roadkill tried to take a chunk out of the judge's shin. His owner yanked sharply on his choke chain.

"Ugly is as ugly does," said Madam Yang, for my ears only.

The judge pointed first at Madam Yang and asked people to clap for her. The applause was loud, but I wasn't sure it was enough.

Then he pointed at Roadkill. The crowd went wild, clapping even harder when Roadkill tried to bite the judge again.

In the end, Madam Yang got twenty-five dollars for being runner-up, and I got a T-shirt with the station's name on the front. Dr. Cotter's bill was $26.95, so I didn't have to break my piggy bank. Natalie said she'd split the difference with me.

As we left Center Court we had to walk by an ice-cream parlor. Outside, sitting on a bench, were my mom and Dr. Cotter, each with a double scoop ice-cream cone.

I stopped dead in my tracks and Natalie bumped into me from behind. She started to ask a question, but I shushed her and pointed. There they were, my mom and Dr. Cotter, taking a lick when the drips threatened to get out of hand, but mostly talking, Dr. Cotter making broad gestures with his hands—and almost losing his ice cream— and Mom, laughing at whatever he was saying.

Natalie, Madam Yang, and I turned around and ducked into a store across the way. The manager spotted us, but Madam Yang blew smoke at her and hid under a sale table. The woman rubbed her eyes in confusion. Natalie and I pretended to be interested in ladies' shoes. Of course, what really interested me was what my mom was doing with the local vet. If Mom had seen us, maybe we could have explained the dragon away as Natalie's pet, but I didn't want to try. I had this weird feeling Dr. Cotter might side with me, and I didn't know how I felt about that.

Then I had an even weirder feeling that I could have danced naked in front of them and they wouldn't have seen me.

My suspicions were confirmed when the little girl with the guinea pig approached them. She had to tug on Dr. Cotter's sleeve to get his attention. I guess she knew him already. Handing his ice-cream cone to my mom, he took the guinea pig. Then he played a little game with the kid, turning her pet first one way, then the other, pretending he didn't know one end from the other. Finally he borrowed one of the barrettes from her hair and clipped it to one end of the guinea pig.

That's when we left.

Natalie brought over her share of the money later and invited me to go swimming.

"So what's this with your mom and Dr. Cotter?"

"What's this what?" I answered with a question.

"You know. Sitting on benches . . . eating ice cream together . . ."

If that wasn't enough, Madam Yang observed that Dr. Cotter didn't look froggy at all, and she and Natalie collapsed into giggles, the dragon snorting smoke all over the place.

Suddenly I'd had enough. "I don't know what you're talking about. Not my mom . . . You don't know anything." Natalie grinned, and if she'd been Santiago, I would have slugged her. "You're seeing things that aren't there!"

"Is she?" Madam Yang asked. I could have sworn she winked at Natalie.

I could feel my face getting hot. "Why don't you both leave and go do something useful for a change . . . like . . . like weld Natalie's braces together so she can't say stupid things!" I snarled like a dragon and stomped out. I went and holed up in my room.

Over dinner, which I only picked at, my mom wondered how my shirt got so stretched out. I didn't know what to tell her, so I didn't say anything.

She's not the only one who can keep a secret.

Chapter 9

Dragons Will
Make You Crazy

Early next morning, before it got hot, I pedaled over to the pet clinic. The bill needed settling. So did my stomach, still doing loop-the-loops thinking about my mom and the vet.

No one answered when I knocked at the front door, but Dr. Cotter himself opened the side entrance.

"Rick, what a nice surprise! I've been meaning to ask you how your, er, big lizard's doing, but I can see for myself she's fine."

I spun around. Madam Yang smiled up at me. "Uh, the *big, fat* lizard is fine," I said hastily. "I'm keeping her away from junk food. She doesn't get any."

Madam Yang growled.

Dr. Cotter stepped back. "Have you told your mom about her yet?"

"Not quite yet. I'm not sure she'd understand."

"You might be surprised. I think she's kind of a special lady." He looked embarrassed, as if he'd said too much. There was a short silence.

I held out the prize money. "I came to pay you for taking care of her, I mean, Madam Yang."

Dr. Cotter put his hands in his pockets. "This is a lot of money, Rick. Maybe we could make a deal instead. I could use a little help on Friday afternoons, while I catch up on paperwork. School is starting soon. And you like animals, right? You could come by after school."

"What would I be doing?"

"Let me show you around. Should we put Madam Yang on a leash?"

"That's a good idea," I managed to say with a straight face. "You'd better let me put it on.

"Behave," I hissed to the dragon. She snorted, but didn't bite off my fingers. So then I got a tour, everything from supplies to the surgery.

Near the end, the vet stopped to pet a cat in a cage along the wall. "Meet Rascal. He got in a fight again. He's probably in once a month, this time with not one but two infected ears. He's ready to go home this morning." Dr. Cotter's hands were large and capable, but gentle with the tomcat, who purred his thanks. The phone rang and the vet excused himself.

"So what's your problem with him?" Madam Yang whispered. "He takes good care of little furry animals."

"He seems like a nice guy, but—"

"But what? You want your mom to be alone the rest of her life?"

"No! I mean, she won't be! She'll have me!"

Madam Yang just rolled her eyes because Dr. Cotter was calling me. We trooped into his office. He finished explaining what I'd be doing. "Anyway, Rick, it wouldn't be the same thing every week, because I never know what's going to walk in the door, on four legs or two. So, what do you say?"

Part of me wanted to be cautious, but it sounded like fun. "I'll have to ask my mom."

"Sure, ask Syl—er, your mother. If she has any questions, she can call me. See you next Friday, then?"

"*Hasta viernes,*" I said.

The dragon and I ended up at Natalie's that afternoon. I'd tried to stay mad at Natalie over what she'd said about my mom and Dr. Cotter, but you can't stay mad at her. And I think Madam Yang meant well.

We were stuck in Ben's room, watching him. We couldn't go swimming until their mom came back from the dentist's. We couldn't go to my house because my mom was there. If it were just Nat and me, we'd have hopped on our bikes, but there was Ben and his slow-motion training wheels to consider.

"It's no fair!" Ben whined. "I never get to go anywhere I want."

He had a point. When you're his age, you're not given lots of choices. Your parents can drag you anywhere they want and you have to go. Hey, my mom moved me from San Diego to Tucson and I'm almost twelve.

I was thinking about forgiving her.

"Perhaps . . ." said Madam Yang. She got this dreamy look in her eyes.

Uh-oh, I thought.

Natalie caught on quick. "Oh, no, you don't. Not my little brother. I'm responsible for him."

"I get to go someplace Natalie doesn't?" Ben asked, his eyes dancing. "I pick what I want?"

"In your dreams," Natalie put in. "You're not going anywhere without me."

Ben looked mutinous.

Madam Yang yawned. "Well, it wouldn't have to be anywhere dangerous, not even anyplace real."

"In my 'magination?" Ben asked. He looked disappointed.

The dragon nodded.

"How can you do that?" I demanded.

For once, she gave me a straight answer. I think. "Dragons are creatures of myth, Rick. We exist 'in your dreams,' so it's not surprising we can take you there." Madam Yang crossed her forelegs and considered her nails. "Natalie, does your mom have any nail polish?"

We weren't going to be diverted.

"It's not a good idea," I said.

"Oh, pish posh." Madam Yang waved away our objections like so many gnats. "There will be safeguards, of course."

"Like before?" Natalie asked.

Madam Yang ignored her. She touched Ben's shoulder. "Now, close your eyes. Concentrate on where you'd like to be."

Natalie and I lunged for the dragon's tail. Next thing you know, boom, we're sitting on the bumpy floor of Ben's Lego castle.

Actually we were locked in the dungeon. To make matters worse, Madam Yang and Ben were missing.

Over in the corner, whoever-it-was had died. The skeleton could have slipped his shackles now, thin as he was, but not in real life. Luckily all his remains were plastic.

"It's Mr. Bones," observed Natalie.

"What?" I said.

"Ben got him for his birthday. He put him together like a puzzle. You know: The leg bone's connected to the thigh bone. . . . There's this orange pedestal thingy he's supposed to stand on, but it got lost."

Mr. Bones was not to scale. If he'd been able to stand up, I ball-parked he'd be twice my height. "Well, either he's grown or we've shrunk."

"Same difference. That darn dragon!" Natalie got up and tried to kick in the door. Like the walls, it was constructed of bricks, all different colors. Ben built solidly. Though hollow, those little bricks are strong. Natalie soon gave up in disgust.

The wall behind me began to heat up. I thought I was imagining it, but then the bricks got so hot I had to move. Whole blocks were melting, puddling like melted crayons. A tongue of flame shot through the opening.

"Madam Yang!"

She put a talon on her lips. "Don't say anything! Just follow me."

Natalie immediately crawled through the hole, but I thought of something I wanted to do first. Pulling Mr. Bones out of his shackles, I dragged him to the hole, crawled through, and propped him up in front of it. A casual glance from the guard, if there was one, wouldn't give our escape away.

Outside, Natalie asked Madam Yang where Ben was.

"Don't know," came the unreassuring reply, "but I heard the trumpets blaring a while ago."

Natalie looked concerned, the big sister in her coming out. "We have to find him. This isn't a safe place."

What I knew about the Middle Ages could have fit into a couple of comic books—actually, that's where I'd learned most of what little I did know. Knights and ladies, peasants and serfs—it had been a real bad-news time. Didn't they have the plague and all that? I would keep that pleasant little thought to myself.

"Madam Yang, how did you know how to find us?" I demanded.

"I sniffed you out."

"Well, then, sniff out Ben."

"It's not that simple." The dragon hesitated. "When I took you before, those were real places, real times. This is something Ben made up. I'm not sure of the rules. You see, they are *his* rules." She looked as confused as I felt.

Just then we heard a noise like thunder, only up close and personal.

"This way." Madam Yang took off, Natalie and me hard on her tail. Racing toward the front of the castle, we steered clear of the moat. None of us wanted to test any theories about plastic crocodiles, or with whatever Ben's imagination had stocked it. We stopped at the corner and peered around. The air smelled smoky, tickling my throat.

"Now, where did he get cannon?" Madam Yang was asking herself. "Is gunpowder even invented yet? This is not altogether logical."

"It came with the set. When we get home, you can write to the manufacturer," said Natalie, totally exasperated with her. "And you'd better get us home soon."

A bunch of plastic men in armor with a battering ram were attacking the castle's main gate. Far above us, his face blackened with smoke, we could see a small figure running around the parapets.

But before Ben could reload, the gate bent inward and the blocks tumbled down. The leader ordered his men to take the castle. They brought Ben out with a rope pinning his arms. His legs were free though, and I saw him kick one of his captors.

The leader took off his helmet. He wore a perpetual plastic smile on his face, but he didn't look nice. With one hand he picked up Ben by the neck of his shirt, holding him at eye level.

"Throw the spratling in the moat," the knight said.

That's when Ben spat in his face.

"Oh, dear, oh, dear," said Madam Yang. "Now he's done it."

Natalie pointed toward the ceiling and whispered urgently to Madam Yang. But even I didn't think Madam Yang could conjure up a total eclipse of the sun without electrocuting herself (it's a lightbulb, okay?), although escaping from the kingdom of Ben's room under cover of darkness seemed like a good plan.

Trouble was, we didn't even have a bad plan.

"It won't work," Madam Yang said. "I told you before, I'm not Aladdin's genie. And besides, it's Against the Rules."

I was beginning to hate that phrase.

"Well, break them!" Natalie put her hands on her hips. "You said there were going to be safe-guards!"

Meanwhile the leader was looking at Ben like he'd stepped in something nasty. "You dare to challenge me?"

"You bet," said Ben. The kid operated with more courage than brains.

That was Natalie's limit. She came running out. "You can't, he's just a kid!"

The leader looked her over. "It is a lawful chal-lenge. Stay out of the way."

"Ben, don't!" Natalie yelled out, before a hand clamped down over her mouth.

They picked broadswords. Ben was untied and given a shield. The leader took off his armor and chain mail to make it fair, as fair as it can be when a grown man duels with a little boy. I didn't think Ben could even pick his sword up, but I'd forgot-ten they were plastic. I wondered how sharp the edges could be. I did know that it hurts like heck when you step on Legos barefoot.

"Madam Yang, you've got to do something," I urged. "Ben could get hurt."

"Not seriously," came her answer. Then doubt-fully, "At least I don't think so."

"Go fry him or something!"

"Rick, remember, he's a knight. They *live* to kill dragons. I don't think Ben will get hurt; this is, after all, his fantasy, but dragon slaying is certainly within bounds. Let's work on creating a diversion, shall we?"

Ben and the leader began whacking away. What Ben missed out on in height, he made up for in speed. The leader's flat feet slipped on the carpet, while Ben's bare feet kept their purchase. Ben got a couple of quick jabs in at the leader's knees. Then the knight's sword came down hard on Ben's shoulder. Luckily, Ben's shield took the brunt of the blow. Ben staggered back.

Diversion, diversion. Think! Suddenly I had an idea. About time! I made a beeline for the cell.

"Sorry, Mr. Bones," I said. "I'll try and bring it back."

With Madam Yang hyperventilating beside me, making lots of smoke, I grabbed the skull, and ran as if Ben's life depended on it. I'm pretty sure it did.

It looked bad. Ben still had his sword, but he'd lost his shield. He was running madly about, just staying out of reach. He couldn't last much longer. Natalie was screaming and so was her captor. Maybe she'd bitten him.

Now for my Hollywood moment.

I nailed my scene. It was better than Boris Karloff, although my dialogue could have been improved. Mr. Bones's skull over my head, I came around the corner and said "Halt!" in my deepest voice. It helped that Death was wearing my black T-shirt and matching sneakers.

"I am Death," I continued, introducing myself. Ben and the leader had stopped fighting and were staring. The leader's knees began to shake. He still wore that smile, but I could smell his fear. A superstitious people in a superstitious age, I thought: I'll give them something to be superstitious about.

"Today is not a good day to die," I said, with mental apologies to Worf. "If you cut down this child, I will be your next challenger. I ask you this one question: Dost thou feel lucky? Because no one cheats Death."

The leader threw down his sword and prostrated himself on the carpet. All the other knights followed suit. Ben carefully set down his sword. He hadn't recognized me.

"Beware if you touch this child. For he is the . . . the . . . true king." I slowly backed away, not turning until I was screened by the castle. I doffed the skull to see better.

The leader was kneeling before Ben.

"I pledge myself and my men to you, lord. Forever from this day forward shall we serve you."

"Please get the guys to fix the castle door, then. Oh, and unhand my sister, the Lady Natalie." As soon as she was free, Natalie rushed over and hugged him.

Once the men were busy working on the blocks, Natalie beckoned, and the three of us scooted inside. In the Great Hall, the table had been set for a banquet. There was food in the trenchers, and I was hungry, but I don't do plastic.

Soon we were standing on the parapets, surveying the kingdom of Ben's room, the mountains of dirty clothes, the rockslides of toys left anywhere, the high cliffs of his bed just beyond the far castle wall. Below us, the plastic men were tamping together blocks to rebuild the castle's entrance. One called to his mates for more red blocks. Madam Yang fluttered up to join us.

"Now, your majesty?" said Madam Yang.

"Do we have to?" Ben pleaded.

"Remember your nightmare last week?" Natalie asked. "The humongous, hungry *T. rexes?*" This wasn't the Jurassic, but anything could happen in Ben's imagination. So we all grabbed Madam Yang, Ben closed his eyes in concentration, and just like that, we were back. The mountains had shrunk down to half a laundry load's worth of dirty clothes, the toys were in danger of being crunched underfoot, and the bed was a bed again. Little plastic men stood frozen by the castle entrance.

"Wow!" said Ben. "Do it again!"

"I am in need of a cup of tea," said Madam Yang grimly. She looked wrung out. "That did not turn out the way I expected, not even quite."

Natalie gave her an I-told-you-so look. Madam Yang's ears flattened, but for once she didn't say anything.

We all had a cup of tea spiked with ginger. It seemed appropriate, Merrie Olde Englande and all. Madam Yang didn't exactly apologize, but she did say she was quite relieved that all had turned out well.

Ben complained, "I didn't get a round table, like King Arthur." Natalie soothed him, saying it would have been hard to build out of rectangular bricks anyway. He wandered on back to his room. My guess is some plastic men were about to be tortured in the dungeon.

Chapter 10

Madam Yang
Bends the Rules

Back at my house, Madam Yang cheered up considerably. "I had no idea what it is like to be a parent. *In loco parentis,* that is. Ben must drive his parents loco. A five-year-old is a dangerous thing. Do you think it could be he watches too much television?" She was still shaking her head over the incident. "But you, Rick, you performed admirably. I have great hopes for you. You should be very pleased with yourself."

"About what?" I'd found a note on the kitchen table from my mom, saying she'd gone out with Evan Cotter. I'd crumpled it up before the dragon could read it, but she looked at me like she had it figured out. I'm so transparent she can see right through me, I guess.

Instead of answering, she started sniffing lazily around the floor.

"Smell any cowboy beans?" I asked sarcastically.

Madam Yang had stopped near the wall between the table and the refrigerator. She called me over. I went, but reluctantly. The dragon tugged on the hem of my shorts. "Here," she said, "smell here."

I got down on my hands and knees, grateful not to have an audience, and sniffed. "I don't smell anything. What do you smell?"

"Bananas," she said.

"Bananas?" Madam Yang was making *me* bananas.

"Look, Rick, this is a little bit Against the Rules—"

"A little bit?"

"Okay, not a little bit. Totally Against Them. There." She smiled, deliberately showing her teeth. "But this smell—"

"Bananas," I repeated.

"Right, bananas, is important."

"I didn't know people ate bananas a hundred and fifty years ago."

"They didn't, at least not here," she snapped. "Look," she gave up, exasperated. "Put your hand here, close your eyes and concentrate."

This I was not about to do. I'd had enough for today of time-slipping, imagination-hopping, or whatever you want to call it. I sat up and shook my head.

"You'll just be an occupant, not a participant in this time, I promise," said Madam Yang. "No one will be able to see you."

"What time?" I wavered, but curiosity is a powerful force and finally I put my hand down on the middle of the tile. "Here?"

"There," the dragon said. "Just close your eyes. I'll do the concentrating."

My hand was in the middle of something gross. I opened my eyes and said, "Yuck! What is this?"

"Banana," said the dragon. "Mushy banana."

But how did it get on the floor? I wiped my hand on my shorts and looked up. I saw two chubby feet dangling from chubby legs attached to a chubby baby sitting in a high chair. She was crooning to herself and squishing banana slices between her fingers. From time to time, she would fling one to the floor. I backed up out of range, though she didn't seem to see me.

Then the sliding door opened and a man stepped in. It was Dr. Cotter. He, too, ignored us, as if Madam Yang and I weren't even there. It was getting weirder. The baby looked up from her mess and started saying, "Ick! Ick!"

Dr. Cotter smiled and spoke to her, as if she could understand everything he said. "Ick—I mean Rick—Rick will be here soon. He and Mama are getting his driver's permit. And it looks like I'm going to give you a bath." He unhitched her from the high chair and took her down the hall toward the bathroom, bouncing her as he went. "That's my girl who looooves bananas," I heard him sing as the bathroom door closed.

Madam Yang took my hand and told me to close my eyes.

When I reopened them, we were back in the kitchen minus the bananas and the high chair.

"What was that?" I asked.

"You don't know?" asked the dragon. She looked genuinely puzzled. "Why, you just caught a glimpse of the future, Rick. Your future."

I sat down in the closest chair, trusting its legs but not mine.

Madam Yang poured me some water. "Drink," she said.

I sipped a little but still felt woozy. "That's my future?"

"It can be," the dragon said. She looked smug. "It's one of a number of possible futures for you, the one with the highest probability at the moment, that is, if you don't blow it."

"What do you mean, blow it?"

"Think about it," the dragon said, then she headed for my room and the closet.

I did think. I thought so hard, steam probably came out of my ears. When I was done, I went and sat on the couch, waiting for Dr. Cotter to bring my mom home.

That's right, I said home. Tucson, Arizona 85749.

Chapter 11

Please Don't Eat
the Princess

"Incredibly bad news," said Natalie. She snapped
the rubber bands on her braces for emphasis. The
two of us were sitting in the hammock in my backyard, kicking up dirt with our toes as we swung
lazily back and forth. Madam Yang dozed by the
sliding glass door to the kitchen, apparently worn
out from our travels yesterday. At least, I thought
so at the time.

"You have to watch Ben again?" Actually,
Natalie's little brother's not so bad. After watching him in action yesterday I realized he's the kind
of kid you want on your side. Besides, if he pes-
tered us too much, Natalie and I could count on
Madam Yang being willing to read to him. She
owed us. As I watched, Madam Yang yawned.

"No, worse than that," Natalie informed me. "My cousin Olivia's coming for a visit. You don't know what she's like. You should see her. She's nine years old and wears all these frilly dresses and she talks like she's a queen or something. She competes in beauty pageants and she never lets you forget that she's the reigning Little Miss Princess. She's won that one twice."

I couldn't imagine wanting to compete in a beauty pageant. The ugly pet contest had gotten that out of my system.

"So when's her majesty coming?"

"This afternoon, and Mom and Dad say I have to be nice to her." She looked downright glum.

At lunchtime Natalie went home, but she came back around three thirty.

"I had to get away for a while. I'm making cookies for Princess Olivia—it was her idea, but, of course, she doesn't know where anything is—and I need to borrow some eggs."

"You can bring us back some cookies. I bet Madam Yang would like some."

"Do you think?"

"You saw her with the marshmallows."

But when we looked for the dragon, she was nowhere to be found. Fat Boy came out and twined himself around my legs. That was curious. Usually we only saw him when the dragon was safely napping in my closet. Then I noticed the sliding glass door was ajar.

"Natalie, have you seen Madam Yang recently?"

"No, why should I? She lives with you."

A quick search turned up nada.

I ran to get my bike, Natalie right behind me.

"What's with you?" she called out.

"I've got a bad feeling about this," I said. "A real bad feeling. I hope I'm not right."

But I was. Madam Yang had treed Olivia in Natalie's backyard. Olivia kept trying to climb higher, but the branches were getting narrower and starting to bend lower. Her ruffled dress was torn and her ringletted blonde hair had twigs in it. You could see she'd been crying.

"Madam Yang! Get away from that tree!"

Madam Yang briefly turned away from Olivia and looked at me.

"Get the hose, Natalie!"

"That won't be necessary," Madam Yang huffed. "If I singe the branches, she'll come down."

"No, I won't!" screamed Olivia. "Ew! Get away from me, you, you, whatever-you-are. Ew! Call 9-1-1!"

I grabbed the dragon's tail and pulled backward with all my strength. She dug her claws into the sun-baked ground.

"Madam Yang, you can't eat her," I pleaded. "She's Natalie's cousin."

The dragon paused and looked from Olivia to Natalie and back again, trying to see a resemblance. "She's not royalty?" she asked, doubt in her voice.

"No," said Natalie firmly. "She's just a royal pain in the—"

Olivia screamed again, this time in anger, and grudgingly the dragon moved away from the tree. Slowly Olivia began to scramble down, her ruffles catching on the miniature thorns of the mesquite. Her dainty feet had barely touched the ground before she made a break for it. She ran for the house, slamming the screen door behind her. We all heard the click as she shot the lock home.

"C'mon, Madam Yang," I said. "Let's go home in case the police show up."

The dragon trotted obediently beside me.

"Pity," I heard her mutter. "She did look fresh, and my stomach is so touchy these days."

"Believe me," Natalie called after us, "she'd have given you a whopper stomachache. Dr. Cotter would have had to pump your stomach."

I turned to Natalie. "You'd better see if Olivia's all right."

"Yeah, I suppose."

Later I called to get the scoop.

"She's fine," said Natalie, "but I had to give her all my Barbies to shut her up."

Somehow I didn't think this would bother Natalie much and I told her so. She just didn't look like a girl who adored fashion dolls. Now, maybe if there were an Inventor Barbie . . .

Surprisingly, she disagreed with me. "I was going to use them as crash dummies in a scale model—my parents won't let me use Ben anymore. I think you'd better keep Madam Yang under wraps for a while."

"It could have been really bad," I agreed.

"You know what? I don't think so. One bite of Olivia would have done her in. Remember how Madam Yang told us she hates artificial sweeteners? That's all Olivia is, artificially sweet, at least when someone's looking."

"Ew," I said.

Next morning we all met in Natalie's workshop. Natalie had hung a "Girl Thinking! Do Not Disturb!" sign from the doorknob.

"I think the time has come for me to move on." Madam Yang held up her talons, shushing any objections. "I realize the, er, Olivia incident could have been a sticky one to explain. Rule number one: Don't ever eat your assignment or anyone close to him. At Dragonwerks, excuses like 'Sorry, I ate my homework' just don't fly. Possibly if someone hadn't rationed my marshmallows—not that I'm naming names—Olivia wouldn't have had that little problem. Anyway," here she looked meaningfully my way, "I think I've accomplished what I set out to do. So it's for the best."

"What's the second rule?" Natalie asked.

"I think she makes them up as she goes along," I whispered, "and if she doesn't want to do something, it's Against the Rules."

The dragon winked at me. "The second rule is: Don't tell anyone the rules."

"Madam Yang, you are a pest!" I said.

She smiled at me. "I'm trained to be an irritant, the grain of sand in the oyster that produces the pearl, so I'll take that as a compliment." Then she fanned out travel brochures like a deck of cards on Natalie's workbench. "Now, not that I get to pick my next assignment, you understand," she said. "But sometimes, with my seniority, I do get to choose between several options. And I am about due for a vacation. I could certainly use one."

The dragon pointed to a picture of a white wedding cake of a castle, set against a dark emerald forest. "Take that one. It's Neuschwanstein in Bavaria. I do like castles—real ones—and this is one of the best. The king who built it was eccentric, if I remember my history. Don't know about the princess situation, though," Madam Yang said doubtfully. "I think that line died out."

"You really should think about giving up on princesses," observed Natalie. "I mean, it's obvious that as a food source, you can't count on having one around. If you insist on a genuine princess, then you'll have to deal with all the bodyguards and so on. If I were you, I'd look into becoming a vegetarian."

"Or just eat bad guys," said Ben, trying to be helpful.

"Bad guys?" Madam Yang pulled on her left earring, thinking about it.

"Yeah, you could work for the CIA as an undercover operative," I added.

Madam Yang looked from Natalie to Ben to me. "If you hang around a castle long enough, royalty always turns up. Finding a suitable meal isn't quite the problem you might think, although I will readily admit that dragons probably have contributed to princesses becoming an endangered species. But, eating 'bad guys?' I think you have been watching too many adventure shows on television, my dears. Besides, there are strict rules about changing the course of history. I can't just go around eating people indiscriminately. Princesses are standard fare; people expect them to be eaten by dragons, so that's all right. Also, you have to consider my digestion. I'm sure a 'bad guy' wouldn't be good for me."

"You could just toast 'em," I said, unwilling to give up my image of saving the world from evil. "Make it look like an accident?"

Madam Yang just looked at me. "I think you're blowing smoke, young man. Still, I could take it up with my superiors. Sometimes the appropriate stimulus can change things for the good." At my blank look, she added, "Change is good, wouldn't you say? Shakes things up?"

I thought about that one. In the past two weeks, I'd moved to Tucson, acquired a dragon, helped two star-crossed lovers escape to Alta California, almost been eaten by another dragon, won second prize in an ugly pet contest, played dead so that Ben would live, rescued a nine-year-old princess from certain death (and Madam Yang from certain stomach upset). I'd even caught a glimpse of my own future if I didn't mess it up. It was a lot. I could just about wish for school to start so things could settle down.

Well, not quite.

I'd kept the bit about Ick and the bananas to myself. I knew Natalie would be interested, but it was my secret, and I didn't have to share it. Not yet, anyway. It wasn't something I should talk about, like broadcasting your wish before you blow out the birthday candles. Dr. Cotter, Evan, I mean, was more than nice and just maybe, he's what Mom and I'd been missing. Time would tell.

For certain, I wouldn't have missed having a dragon around for the world. I gave Madam Yang a quick fierce hug. I felt her breath hot on my cheek, but I didn't mind.

"Don't go," I whispered.

"I'll miss you, too, Rick," she whispered back, "but I don't fit in here and you, I think you do now. Can you see that?"

I did. I guess if I only move every eleven years I might be able to stand it.

We said good-bye to Madam Yang that night. Armed with a telescope, a clear moonless night, and an excuse that we were going stargazing for comets, we gathered in my backyard. Madam Yang gave us each a quick embrace, then stepped back.

"I don't like long good-byes—they're bores, and besides, I may come back and see you sometime," Madam Yang told us. "But I do have something to say to each of you. Ben, I want you to stay away from human pincushion situations, at least until you have a few dozen fencing lessons under your sword belt." Ben looked puzzled, but nodded anyway. The dragon added, "Ask your mom.

"Now then, Natalie, of course you'll keep up those inventions. They'll take you far. You didn't hear it from me, but you may want to investigate the wizard's wand as a power source." At Natalie's guilty look, she said, "Yes, I saw you take it. I don't have to tell you to be careful. But remember, use it only as a power source. Don't go fooling around with magic on your own. That's all I need, to have the Wizards' Guild on my tail. Understand?" Natalie nodded.

Then the dragon turned to me. "And Rick . . . We understand each other, don't we? Despite our fearsome reputation, by and large, people like dragons. I think there's a little dragon in you. Let it out when you need to." Here the dragon broke off. She leaned into my shirt and took a deep sniff. "You know what? Yes. Unmistakably, your future smells of peanut butter!"

Madam Yang unfurled her wings and fluttered off into the night sky, and for a long time we could see her as she breathed fire to illuminate her flight. It was better than Halley's comet, Shoemaker-Levy, and Hale-Bopp all rolled together, but I still had a lump in my throat as big as Jupiter.

Chapter 12

Starting Over

Natalie showed up at my place soon after the breakfast I hadn't felt like eating. Madam Yang had flown away two nights ago, and yesterday Dragonwerks had finally come through with the new heating system—the real one. Once we got the crate open and could see inside, Mom got all excited. I tried hard, but I just couldn't. After all, a furnace, even a superefficient one, doesn't compare to a dragon.

I hadn't known how much I'd miss Madam Yang. She'd clued me in that I didn't need to keep everything bottled up inside. To trust my sometimes dragonlike feelings—and people, too. What was it she'd said, when we first met? "Some kids need fairy godmothers. Others need dragons."

Yeah, right—to breathe fire down their shorts.

But you know what? It had worked.

In a way, Madam Yang had been my fairy god-mother, except for the part about a happy ending. I mean, if you believe Cinderella and her prince didn't fight after they got married, there's this desert oasis in my backyard I'd like to sell you. I had to *make* my own happy ending.

And that's what was bothering me.

Natalie punched me in the shoulder, not too hard, but it got my attention. "You know what your problem is? You worry too much." She was like a Smiley-face poster child, grinning and jumping up and down with a secret she couldn't contain for long.

"Where's your mom?" she asked. "In her dark-room?"

"No, no, she's gone out with Dr. Cotter—I mean Evan." I'd been asked to come along, but figured they needed some time alone.

"That's good. I have something to show you," Natalie said. "For your eyes only." She dug into her backpack and pulled out a battered green book. "Check out the title."

Most of the gilt in the ornate script had flaked off long ago, but I finally made it out. *Raising Dragons.* I looked at Natalie.

"It's the book Marcella put on reserve at the library. Remember, when Madam Yang was sick?" Then, more impatiently, "Don't you get it? Look!"

She riffled through the first couple pages and pointed at the dedication. "There."

The acknowledgment read: "For Rick, who has courage but still needs faith . . . I believe in you.—M.Y." Wonderingly, I turned the page. "'Chapter 1,'" I read aloud. "'Before hatching, a dragon's egg must be kept in a cool, dark place, not damp . . .'"

Natalie locked eyes with me. "Are you thinking what I'm thinking?"

"No way, it couldn't be . . ." I sputtered.

"Think about it. She had problems with her stomach. She slept a lot. Just like my mom with Ben."

"It could be different with dragons."

"Are you sure?"

I was never totally sure about anything with dragons. "But would she trust us with something like that?"

"I think she would," said Natalie, "and I think I know where."

"The darkroom!" we yelled at the same time.

At the back of the bottom cupboard, there was something hard, about baseball size. The stiff paper wrapped around it crackled.

I took a deep breath. "Let's go out in the back-yard."

"Take it out in the sun, Rick," Natalie suggested.

"Do you think that's a good idea?"

"Well, I did skim the first couple pages—" She grinned at me.

Trust Natalie. I couldn't help but grin back.

Sunlight glinted off the metal skin of the dome. Like mercury in a glass thermometer, its surface looked shiny and liquid at the same time. The egg, for that's what it was, heated up in the sun.

We heard a ticking sound, then a crack. The egg began to open from inside. Amid a shower of sparks, a small green head poked out, eyes shut tight against the glare. Its tiny mouth opened, and a tongue of flame shot out.

I reached out my hand.